THE MIDWINTERS

The Midwinters

Julie Rainsbury

First Impression – 2005

ISBN 1 84323 568 4

© Julie Rainsbury, 2005

Julie Rainsbury has asserted her right under the
Copyright, Designs and Patents Act, 1988,
to be identified as Author of this Work.

This book is published with the financial support of the
Welsh Books Council.

Printed in Wales at
Gomer Press, Llandysul, Ceredigion SA44 4JL

Chapter 1

She came out of the darkness at the dead end of the year, when all the hope and glitter of celebration had gone, when the whole town crouched low around the bay and braced itself for the long haul, the worst of winter. Grey stone, grey slate, grey skies. Even the sea was grey – sleek yet harsh – cold as gunmetal. Not that I've ever touched gunmetal, of course, but you can imagine its shiver, can't you?

We were taking down the skeleton of the tree and Mam was on her knees with a dustpan, brushing up pine needles, because the Hoover was on the blink.

'Don't ever let me be tempted again,' she moaned. 'Blow romantic and proper, blow paying out for one with roots that we can plant in the garden. I always forget to water them and then they end up like this – dead as a doornail and with enough mess stuck in the carpet to make sure we'll still be walking on pins come August. Next year we're having plastic or maybe metallic – you know, silver or gold or shiny purple – anyway, one of those with bows or fir cones already stuck in place so all you've got to do is fold the whole thing away in a box. Blow your dad saying a real one'll look lovely . . . be perfect . . . make the best Christmas ever . . . '

Mam suddenly clattered the brush into the dustpan,

scattering half the pine needles she'd already collected. Their scent filled the room but she'd made us jump.

'I'll go and get your tea ready,' she said, and it's funny how ordinary words can sound so angry.

The door slammed behind her. She probably didn't mean to slam it. After all, pine needles and a cranky Hoover weren't exactly our fault. That door handle had always been loose and it slipped from your hand sometimes. I expect that's what it was. Before he left, Dad had kept on promising to fix it but somehow he never did. It was just another thing we were stuck with, another thing we had to learn to live with. Sioned started to cry though. Anything can set Sioned off. She was only three back then, I know, but she was a right cry-baby. I don't cry and, even when I was three, I bet I wasn't such a tap as Sioned. I'm miles older than she is. I was already eleven when all this happened and I'm twelve now. Besides, boys don't cry like girls, do they? Not about soppy things like slamming, anyway. Not in front of people. Not in the daytime.

I picked Sioned up and dumped her on the sofa. I gave her the star from the top of the tree to play with. She liked the star, twisting its points round and round between her fingers, forgetting her tears. The star was already a bit bent and bald at the back where the shine had worn off – so even Sioned couldn't do it much more harm.

I went on wrapping baubles in kitchen paper and shaking the dust out of tinsel before I coiled it away. It would have meant bad luck if the decorations weren't all packed up by the end of the day. We'd had enough bad luck. I wasn't about to risk any more.

Sioned had started singing to her star, 'Twinkle, twinkle . . .' but the song sounded sad, her voice so thin and high, and there was no light on in the room to spark her star into life. Taking decorations down was making me feel more and more fed up. It wasn't that Christmas had been great – it was just that I had thought it might be. Well, not great exactly, of course I hadn't expected that. Not even good either, I suppose. I'd really just hoped for better – better than usual, if you know what I mean.

All at once, Christmas was in the past. We'd been tipped into another year and the house, stripped back to normal, to reality, seemed even bleaker than before. Every grubby mark, every worn patch, every battered edge appeared worse and more obvious. It's not that I care about paint-work or housekeeping and daft stuff like that, which is just as well as Mam certainly doesn't, but I used to do a lot of staring and a lot of wondering at that time. I was watchful. I noticed details, little changes, hidden meanings. I was always trying to work things out, make them right. Sometimes you can think so much your head hurts, can't you? Sometimes thinking makes your head want to explode.

I pulled some more tinsel down from the tree. The garlands were beginning to tarnish, their brightness spotted and spoilt by flecks as grey as the day outside. I picked up the dullest strands and carried them to the window to check whether they were worth saving.

That's when I saw her for the first time. She came out of the darkness. Appeared, sudden as sea mist, between the late afternoon shadows of corner house and pub at the top of our street. She was green. I don't mean her face or anything like that. She wasn't an alien. She wasn't that weird. But you could say she was strange. In fact, she was very strange, extremely odd, definitely funny . . . funny peculiar not funny ha-ha . . . and I knew that at once.

She was dressed completely in green, from the top of her flounce-feathered hat to the pointy-toed tips of her leaf-patterned boots. She came dancing down the hill through the rivulets of rain that swirled in the gutters. Water spattered, spilled, spurted – glistened around her. Her cape spun out as she twirled. Her ropes of beads, jade and pearl, rippled and chinked like stones under breaking waves. I gazed at her, amazed. As she whirled closer, I saw that more pearls, sprigged with gold, swung from her ears and others clung, milky as moonshine, amongst the greenery of her garments.

Her spinning made me giddy. Sounds – indoor sounds, outdoor sounds – started to fill my head:

Sioned's voice, the chink-clink of beads,
that ever-present rhythm of wave after wave,
pitter and plash of rain and its gurgle into drains,
the microwave's ping as Mam banged plates in the kitchen,
the kettle's whistling, quick dancing footsteps in the street,
toll and chime of rigging as boats rocked in the harbour,
the gas fire's shushed hiss, cars slowing . . . revving away,

clamouring of gulls and crows and a gale gradually rising,
a chorus through the bare-branched trees. Sounds flooded in.
Echoes and chants, poems and spells, lullabies and carols –
their song swelled and ebbed, swelled and ebbed, swelled . . .

A double thump as the green woman dropped her bulging bags on the bench opposite our front door.

'Celyn!'

Her call wasn't loud yet it cut across all other noise. I blinked. My head emptied.

'Celyn! Come on!'

And that's when I saw her. The other one. The child. She came out of the darkness, clothed in evergreen like her mother. Sharp-faced, sharp-kneed and elbowed. Dancing down through the town, wilder than our winter winds, wilder than our wildest weather. Even now, I find it hard to describe her: ragamuffin, flibbertigibbet, tatterdemalion. Her bobbed hair blazed – blood red, berry bright.

The woman laughed at her daughter's dance and gathered her under her cloak, protecting her from the worsening downpour. The woman looked about her. Day was fading fast and I noticed that the wide curve of mountains far across the bay was already lost from sight. The woman hugged her daughter to her. She glanced upwards and the street lamp clicked on above them. The woman turned her head. Lamps flickered into a chain of light up the street towards the amusement arcade. The woman turned her head again. Lamps flickered into a necklace of light down the street towards the harbour. I told myself it was the sort of thing that happens by accident, but she appeared to control it. The two of them were radiant, glowing through the wet, the grey gloominess, the gathering dusk. They both looked about them. All over the town, one by one, windows brightened.

Sioned chuckled. The star in her hand flashed and sparkled.

'Twinkle, twinkle,' she sang. She was so excited that she sang it over and over, getting louder and louder, faster and faster.

I stepped back from the window. The woman had turned her face towards me, had caught my eye, seen right into our home.

Sioned laughed. She spun the star like some fizzing firework, like a Catherine wheel. The room was illuminated, so suddenly bright that it made me feel dizzy again.

'What's the matter, Hedd? You look as if you've just seen a ghost.'

Mam stood in the doorway, one hand irritably twisting the loose knob, the other on the light switch. I checked her face – red eyes, smudged make-up – so I knew she'd been crying again. But she was smiling as she leant in the doorway – even if it was that tight, sharp smile that made her face appear as if it was about to fall apart into hundreds of pieces like a jigsaw. It was the best smile we got from her then. The only one she gave us.

Mam bustled across the room all brisk and jolly in that bizarre manner parents have when something's wrong but there's no way they're going to explain – so don't ask. She collected the dustpan and brush and then got me to help her carry the bony remains of the tree out into the back yard. We crushed it up into a black rubbish sack and stuffed it into the bottom of the wheelie bin and Mam said that, if we were lucky and kept our fingers crossed, the dustmen might take it and she-for-one would be glad to see the back of it. Mam hates heights so she let me go on the stepladder and stretch up and shuffle the box of decorations back into the loft. She said I was very grown up. She said I was the man of the house. We threw the tarnished tinsel into the swing-bin in the kitchen but Mam let Sioned keep the star.

'How odd,' she said, when Sioned didn't want to let it go. 'The star used to light up like that – but it's been broken for ages. You have it, cariad. It's seen better days anyway. Next year now . . .' She paused and seemed to have to make a determined effort to go on. 'We'll get a new one next year.'

She swung Sioned up into her arms.

'Next year . . . a new star . . . a new start . . .' she murmured into Sioned's hair.

Mam caught me watching her. As I say, I was always staring and wondering then, trying to work things out and it used to drive Mam round the bend. It used to drive Dad mad too. I knew it did but I couldn't stop it.

'Right, Hedd!' she said, plonking Sioned down at the kitchen table. 'Go and draw the curtains in the front room and I'll start to dish up tea. Your favourite – lasagne.'

11

She sang to Sioned, 'Twinkle, twinkle, la–sag–ne . . .'

She was pretending to be happy. She was pretending everything was all right. Have you noticed that adults do that? They act as if you're stupid – as if you don't know anything. Smiling jigsaw smiles, singing star songs, whatever . . . she might have been able to fool Sioned but she couldn't fool me. Boys my age aren't as twp as all that. Boys my age know a thing or two.

I stomped into the sitting room. As I tugged at the heavy curtains, I scanned the street. It had become quite dark, except where the street lamps spilled puddles of light on the wet tarmac making the continued drizzly rain sizzle into fire. From the bay window, I checked out the street up towards the amusement arcade and down towards the harbour – but the green woman and her daughter had vanished.

'Celyn,' I muttered to myself, remembering her spikiness, her berry-coloured hair. I'd never seen the pair of them before but the street already seemed emptier than usual without them.

Then I noticed him, sitting on the bench opposite our house. The woman's bulging bags had disappeared but he sat in their place. The street lamp picked him out as vividly as a spotlight – as if he were on a stage and about to prance into some kind of performance. He didn't move though. He sat still, still as a stone statue. He was a tiny man, small as one of Sioned's dolls. He wore a hat that was a bit like a wizard's, only softer and droopier. His nose was hooked and his mouth gaped as if he was calling to me between the wrought-iron curves of the bench back. One eye open, one eye closed, he winked at me. Not a laughing wink, this wink was terrible. It made his whole face a grimace. Across his knees, he held a stick.

'Mam! . . . Shut up, Sioned! . . . Mam!'

I was in a complete panic.

'There's an awful man outside – a sort of goblin.'

'Gobbling, gobbling las–sag–ne . . .' Sioned sang.

She always goes on if you tell her to stop. Little kids do that, don't they? It's just the way they are – sometimes they're too busy with what they're doing themselves to take any notice and other times they're testing you out to see if you mean it. I was so spooked, I ignored her.

'What d'you mean . . . a goblin?'

Mam came to the window but I could already tell she didn't believe me.

'Are you quite sure now?' She poked me teasingly in the ribs. 'It might be a fairy, a pixie, a sprite or even an elf. It could be a scout for a whole troop of Tylwyth Teg about to invade from those famous invisible islands, the ones your dad was always going on about, beyond the bay. After all, any of those, even if they existed, are VERY likely to have nothing better to do than lurk about . . . in our street . . . on a winter evening . . . in the pouring rain. Are you certain it's just an ordinary goblin, not a hobgoblin? Come on, don't be so daft. You must be imagining things, Hedd!'

Why do people say that? They mean nothing's there or they mean nothing's wrong but sometimes they're not telling the truth and what they're really saying is they don't want to talk about it. I don't think that's

13

fair. When they do that, things worry you even more. I wasn't going to put up with it this time, though. I was too frightened. I took a deep breath.

'No, it's really there, Mam. Look, an ugly old man over on the bench. He's small like a garden gnome, only more miserable, more . . . real.'

I pointed. Mam peered. The street lamp flickered, died. She went into the hall and opened the front door.

'Mam!'

I clutched at the back of her T-shirt, tried to stop her, to save her, but she was gone – out into the rough weather, out into the deepening darkness. She crossed the road, walked away from me towards the horrible manikin.

Sioned came hurtling along the hallway wanting to follow Mam. I caught her, held her tight as she wriggled and fussed.

'You've got no shoes on,' I told her. Sioned hates her feet being wet. She loves jumping in puddles but is a right pain if any water splashes on her socks, on her legs, on any part of her. It's the end of the world if her gloves get the slightest bit soggy. No wonder rain rhymes with pain. Rain is a pain with Sioned – again and again and again. Mam says she'll grow out of it. That means she'll improve as she grows older . . . but I think she's getting worse.

Sioned struggled out of my arms and started to scramble into her wellies. She's got pink ones with daisies on. She was putting them on the wrong feet. You wouldn't catch me in wellies like those. I prefer black, or perhaps green like Dad's. I thought about the green woman with her leaf-patterned boots. I pictured those pointy toes skittering through puddles. Grownups don't usually enjoy playing in puddles.

Mam burst back in through the door with the creature in her arms. Her hair was slicked close to her head and water slipped from her elbows – plop, plipplop – onto the tiled floor. She shook her head and droplets sprayed over us all. I shivered.

'It's a puppet.'

'Poppet,' said Sioned, pulling her feet back out of her boots.

'No, a puppet, poppet. It's Mr Punch.'

'Punch?' Sioned stared at the grotesque puppet. Her bottom lip quivered and her eyes were wide.

'Mr Punch. That's his name. He must be part of a Punch and Judy puppet show. See, he's even got his stick.'

'For beating Judy, for beating the baby, for beating Toby-the-dog,' I said. 'I hate Punch and Judy shows. He's foul. What did you bring him in here for?'

Part of me was a bit relieved, of course. And part of me felt a fool for getting it all wrong. A puppet – even a twisted-faced, fierce puppet like Punch – was better than something real, something alive. He was creepy, though. His face was all jutting angles and was painted with crimson blotches on his nose and cheeks. He looked like someone who's been drinking too much beer. His eyes rolled, first one, then the other. They winked at me – as if he had power, as if he knew everything, as if I was useless.

'I wonder who left him there?'

Mam gave Punch a little shake to get the worst of the wet off him.

'He can't have been on the bench for very long, otherwise he'd be even more soaked.'

She examined him carefully.

'He's got very unusual eyes for a Mr Punch. I can't recall ever seeing one with eyes that moved before.'

I felt I'd known all along that the . . . what could I call him? . . . that the . . . thing . . . would be out of the ordinary. His eyes click-clacked . . . and crossed. His arm slid from Mam's grip, making his stick clatter against the umbrella stand.

'Did you see anyone outside earlier, Hedd? Anyone he could belong to?'

'No.'

I still don't know why I lied. Perhaps it had been embarrassing enough believing in goblins, without having to explain green people dancing into town from nowhere.

'No one, Mam.'

'We'll have to keep him safe for tonight then and I'll ask around in the morning.'

Sioned reached out tentatively and touched the puppet gently with her little finger. His head lolled towards her and she backed away – uncertain.

'Put him upstairs on top of your wardrobe, Hedd, out of harm's way.'

'Do I have to? Can't he go in Sioned's room or . . . or in the cupboard under the stairs?'

'Sioned might damage him and besides . . .' Mam dropped her voice to a whisper, '. . . you're right, he

16

does look a little bit scary. He might give her nightmares.' She raised her voice to normal again. 'And you couldn't swing a kitten, let alone a cat, in that cupboard.'

'Ple . . . ease, Mam! I don't want him. Can't he go in with you?'

'As if! There's no space in my room with all your dad's boxes packed and stacked up waiting for him to come and collect them – whenever he decides it suits him. Here, take him up now and hurry back down to eat, otherwise we might as well have left the pasta frozen.'

I stopped arguing. I didn't want her going on and on about Dad. I couldn't take Punch into my arms like Mam had though. I couldn't hug him tight and safe against me as I did whenever I lifted Sioned. I loved Sioned – even when she was a nuisance – but I hated Mr Punch. No worries at all if I dropped him. I held him by one of his knobbly hands and trailed him behind me. His head scuffed against the carpeted stairs in a series of muffled bu-bumps.

'Be careful,' said Mam. 'You're as bad as Sioned.'

But I wasn't a toddler like Sioned, was I? I couldn't tell Mam he frightened me, that I was as sure as eggs are eggs he would haunt my dreams too. I wished and wished I'd mentioned the green woman and Celyn. I was sure he must belong to them. After all, he was strange and they were strange and they'd all arrived together – they must be connected.

If I'd told Mam, I thought, *perhaps she'd have searched for them tonight. Or rung around to see if they're staying at one of the pubs or B&Bs or with anyone we know in the town. Then I wouldn't be stuck with him.*

I didn't wait around in my bedroom. I was determined to spend as short a time as possible with the ghastly thing. I stood by the door and simply lobbed the puppet up onto my wardrobe, as far back against the wall as I could manage. Hopefully, I wouldn't be able to see him when I went to bed – and he wouldn't be able to see me. Then I shut the door tight and went straight downstairs for tea.

Chapter 2

Usually I love being in my bedroom – it's my favourite place in the whole world. There are three floors in our house and my room is all on its own, right at the top. It's tucked into the roof-space, cwtshed under the eaves, with beams, slanty-sloped ceilings and the very tiniest of windows overlooking the sea. Before Dad left, my bedroom was the very best place to be. I spent most of my time there. I wasn't lonely. It was good to be out of the way. After all, you can't get roped into arguments if there's no one to argue with, can you? If you keep yourself to yourself, you can't upset people by doing or saying the wrong thing. You can't smile by accident and need that smile wiped off your face. And if you don't have friends for sleep-overs, no one else need ever hear anything and you'll never have to explain or have other people feeling sorry for you. In fact, it's safest to avoid having close friends altogether. That's how I felt then, anyway. And if, late, late into the night, there was a storm outside or a row downstairs, I could push the door shut, pull down the blind and tug the duvet tight, tight over my head, so I could hardly hear at all, until it all blew over.

Dad always called my bedroom 'the crow's nest'. He meant like a look-out high in the rigging of an old-fashioned sailing ship. My dad owned a boat. It wasn't one with a crow's nest, of course, but a fishing boat he'd converted to take tourists out to catch mackerel or round the headland to watch the dolphins and seals. In the school holidays, he often used to take me along with him. He said I was his 'first mate'. You might think that means his best friend because mates are friends but, on a boat, it's someone who's important but not as important as the captain. I liked being my dad's mate. Still, I didn't want my room to be a crow's nest – I hated that name. I didn't want to be a horrid crow-thing. Crows bicker and caw and scrap across our roof slates. They buffet the sky, scraggy as bits of ripped rubbish sack. Their nests bloom high in the trees at the edge of next door's garden – so darkly ugly, so bulbous and tatty. Lots of crows together are called a murder, Dad told me. At first I'd thought he must be having me on, but I checked and it's quite true. A murder of crows. You know, like a gaggle of geese or a flock of sheep or a school of dolphins. They're peculiar, words like that, aren't they? When I was up in my room, I'd often think about them, try to find new ones on the internet – a pride of lions, a shoal of fish. I've still got a notebook with a list of them in it. When you read the list, it sounds as if it's meant to be a poem. I'd curl up in bed and wonder about the person who first stared at a sky full of crows and thought *murder*. You can't imagine it, can you? And it would be hard to make up a more unusual description. Anyhow, crows deserve to be called something nasty. They've certainly always made me feel uneasy, queasy – a bit shaky and sick. I didn't want to think of my bedroom as having any link with crows.

Mam always told Dad to 'give over' when he teased me about it. She made up another name for my bedroom – 'Hedd's hive'. She said it was because I was always up there and, if she called me down or asked what-on-earth I was doing, I'd always just say I was 'busy'.

'Busy, busy bee,' Mam said.

'Buzzy, buzzy bee,' said Sioned.

I didn't mind the name 'hive'. I'd never seen a beehive then but 'hive' sounded safe and cosy and sometimes, when the house was all silent for once, sun poured into the room through my tiny window like honey. So sweet and golden and . . . happy.

Sioned's very keen on honey. Mam buys it for her from the Honey Farm – you've probably seen the signs, Fferm Mêl – up by the coast road. Sioned gets it all over her fingers and licks them one by one instead of wiping them properly. If she thinks nobody's watching, she tries to lick it from her toast too, but that's not at all polite. That's worse than licking your fingers, and Mam's having none of it and tells her off. She always wants to play with the wooden lollipop thing that Mam uses, twirling it to lift honey from the jar. Sioned makes a sticky mess with it though and gets honey in her hair and stuff like that – so she's not allowed to have a go very often.

Lots of bees together are a swarm. 'Swarm' is a sunny-honey word – very different to 'murder'. 'Swarm' sounds . . . well . . . warm and ssssort of ssssleepy. It reminds you of the drone of bees in flight and is similar to the sound of someone snoring. Zzzzzzzwarm. Just right, really, for a bedroom.

On the night when the puppet arrived, I didn't want to go up to my bedroom at all. I did everything I could think of to avoid it.

First of all, I read Sioned three bedtime stories and I would have read her more, except Mam said I was making a rod for my own back and we'd never get her to sleep in a month of Sundays unless I packed it in. Mam's full of sayings like that and I use them too. I enjoy all sorts of sayings, expressions, tongue-twisters, rhymes and so on, don't you? Some of them make you laugh and nearly all of them are interesting. Words can be weird and wonderful . . . but I wasn't very fond of 'rod for your own back'. In fact, to be honest, it made me shudder. It made me remember Mr Punch, hunched with his stick in the dusty shadows on top of my wardrobe.

Once Sioned was in bed and I'd:

taken her a drink of water
and tucked her in
and tucked her in again
and found her favourite teddy
and tucked teddy in
and said: Night-night, sleep tight
make sure the bed bugs don't bite
four times because it makes her giggle
and left her door open just a crack
and turned the landing light on
and given teddy just one more kiss . . .

I hung about downstairs for as long as possible. I helped Mam with the drying-up without being asked. I sat and watched *Coronation Street* with her. I never usually watch that. I hate *Coronation Street*. It just rambles on and on and nothing much ever happens and no one ever goes anywhere except up and down the same old bit of road – and it's been doing that, going on and on, since the year dot, since before I was born, since before Mam was born. I think it's even worse than *Pobol y Cwm* and that's saying something. I prefer programmes with less chatting, ones with more action and adventure in them. I want to escape into stories about far away or imaginary places. Programmes like that are way cool.

Mam finally got suspicious when I asked if she wanted me to make her a nice cup of tea, and whether I could stay up late and watch a DVD – her choice. Big mistake . . . and I could tell at once, from the way Mam stared at me, that I'd blown it. Mam knew, firstly, that I never, ever offer to make cups of tea and, secondly, that I'd never in a million years willingly settle for her choice of film. The DVDs Mam wants are always, without fail, dreadful. We can never agree if we go to hire one out from Spar. I know, simply by looking at the box, that Mam's choice will be useless. Either the cover is pink, which is obviously bad news, or it has the most boring picture in the world on it – usually some woman in a bonnet.

'Time you were in bed,' Mam said in that voice she uses when there's no point discussing it. 'Up the little wooden hill.'

The little wooden hill means the stairs. That's what Dad used to say when I was small, before Sioned was born.

'Off we go – up the little wooden hill.'

And he'd swoop me into his arms and give me a piggy-back all the way. The three of us used to get along all right then – but that was a long time ago.

I dawdled in the bathroom on the first floor, cleaning my teeth with extra-special care, having a very, very good wash and even searching through the airing cupboard for some clean pyjamas. Eventually, Mam came up and told me to get a move on and there was no putting it off any longer.

The stairs that lead further up to my attic room are narrow and steep. They creak and groan to themselves as you walk on them. The ceiling is low over the staircase and there's no window so, even with the light on, it's always a bit dim and dingy. That night, just my luck, the bulb had gone – so I had to creep up carefully in the dark, feeling for the walls on each side of me, as the treads muttered and murmured beneath my feet. The sounds echoed, seemed louder than usual. I imagined a voice calling, *caw . . . caw . . .* like a crow, from deep inside that gobliny, wooden head. A cracked, ghostly voice that rasped towards me from the puppet's gaping mouth.

I ran straight across my room and jumped into bed without switching the light on. Although I curled up with my face tight to the wall, I could still feel the puppet's presence behind me. A draft, cold as the very breath of winter, slid between my shoulder blades. Our house seemed so restless, full of odd clicks, coughs and creakings that I was sure had never been there before. I imagined Mr Punch shuffling forward on his wooden knees to peer at me, leer over me. I shuddered and pulled the duvet over my head. I lay rigid. It was as bad as it used to be, waiting for Dad to come home late. The calm before the storm, I suppose you could call it – when the whole world seems peaceful but you know it's all about to kick off. I lay still for a long time until my arm went dead. I shifted it as slowly and as silently as I could, bit by bit, centimetre by centimetre. Wind moaned in the chimney – like a foghorn, a warning. At last I heard Mam go to bed on the floor below me. The house sighed, was drenched in night. My Man-U clock on the shelf ticked . . . and . . . ticked . . . and . . . ticked. In each pause I kept my fingers crossed, expecting that at any moment, within this minute or the next, something must happen.

I'd been so certain I'd never sleep but, eventually, I did. At once, Mr Punch leaped down from his perch on the wardrobe and invaded my dreams. He jabbered and chortled, his lips clacking like castanets as he jumped the jerkiest of jigs. His caperings cast crazy, shifting shadow-shapes about my room. They loomed larger and larger, swarmed across the ceiling, closed in around me. Punch lashed out with his stick, smashed it into my computer, bashed it through the window pane, crashed my clock to the ground. I cowered against the wall. In my dream, I screamed. I screamed at him to stop. The night was flooded with screaming, bitter as a mouthful of blood.

Then they came out of the darkness, the green woman and Celyn. They circled, tiny and bright, spun a green garland on top of my wardrobe. Their hands fluttered, shimmered against the shadows, like faint sunlight through new leaves. Their hands hypnotized me, lulled me with their spell as they pulled the puppet's strings.

The next morning dawned shiny with everything freshly washed by the rain. My nightmare seemed distant, my fears completely stupid. My clock was safely on the shelf, my window unbroken, my computer hummed happily as usual when I switched it on to check.

How did the green woman and Celyn make me feel peaceful when they were the puppeteers bringing Punch to life? I wondered.

I couldn't work out what the dream had meant. That's the thing with dreams, isn't it? They're nonsensical, all mixed up. It's as if all your different worries or thoughts are thrown into some cauldron and muddled together like . . . like trifle or cawl or stir-fry. The result is something . . . other . . . a right old hotch-potch, a witch's brew.

Perhaps they were trying to control Punch, pull him back? They weren't there when he first moved . . .

I gave up wondering. I stood on my bed and looked over at the wardrobe top. I could see Punch, huddled in a heap in the far corner where I'd flung him the evening before. All crunched up there, he looked harmless, old and broken – quite different to how he had appeared on the bench and in my dream. I shook my head.

You're nutty as a fruitcake, Hedd Williams, I said to myself. *Daft as a brush. How could you ever have been frightened of that thing? He's a cartoon man, a piece of carpentry; the idea of him possessing the slightest smidgen of power is complete codswallop. Look at him, he's about as scary as a crumpet!*

I put on my jeans and a sweatshirt and the new trainers Dad had given me for Christmas. They were not the coolest of trainers because Dad hasn't got much money and I could tell they'd come from the seconds shop. I still liked them though. They were black with yellow flashes and laces, so my feet resembled a plump pair of bees. Mam said I had to write Dad a note on the computer saying – *Thank you for thinking of me at Christmas* – you know, like you do when some ancient relative you've never met sends you a present. She insisted – but it was strange doing a note for Dad. It made him feel far away and as if he didn't belong to me any more. He only lives up at the caravan park, after all. I still think I could have just said 'thanks, Dad' the next time I saw him. It would have been nicer somehow, more . . . normal.

After breakfast, Mam started to get Sioned ready to go into town on the bus. It's always a bit of a palaver getting Sioned tidy, even now, and she was younger then. If you wash her face, she smears something on it. She fidgets while you lace, or button or zip her into clean clothes, and then goes and drips something down them. She fusses about her shoes. She loathes having her hair brushed. She won't put her mittens on, or her hat, or her scarf, or . . . whatever. In other words, she gets thoroughly fed up – and so does everyone else.

I hate shopping. I especially hate shopping with Mam. She goes in everywhere and spends forever and a day walking round and then, if assistants try to help her, she says she's 'just looking'. I ask you! Mam says it's called 'window shopping' but I can't see the point of all that traipsing about. She could look at home on the internet and save herself getting worn out and save Sioned throwing a tantrum and save me from falling off the edge of the world with boredom. I've explained this to her dozens of times but she still takes no notice. Adults are like that, aren't they? Always telling you what to do but never taking on board any good tips themselves.

On that particular morning, it was so sunny after days of rain, so bright after my nightmarish night, that I made a real effort to get out of going.

'Can't I stay behind, Mam?' I was planning to try out my new skateboard on the path above the beach.
'Oh, go on . . . It's a lovely day, far too fine to be stuck on a bus or in a crummy shop.'

'Beach! Beach!'

'Now look what you've started,' said Mam crossly. 'You've set Sioned off and you know how she can badger for Wales once she gets an idea into her head.'

'Badger?' Sioned forgot about the beach and stared hard into the umbrella stand as if she expected a black and white snout to peep out at any moment.

'Of course you can't be left here alone. What if you were run over crossing the road . . . or drowned in the

28

sea . . . or kidnapped . . . or . . . something? I'd never forgive myself.'

'What if . . . what if . . .' Grown-ups are full of 'what ifs', aren't they? Why don't they sort out the bad things that are really happening right under their noses instead of worrying about 'what ifs' that might never happen at all?

'Dad used to let me go off and play by myself. As long as he knew where I'd be . . .'

Mam flushed and twisted Sioned round sharply to do up her coat.

'That's because your father only worried about what he wanted to do. He'd be busy on his blasted boat, leaving you to roam about . . . anything might have . . .'

She caught sight of my face and paused. She buckled Sioned into the pushchair.

'It's not that he didn't care, Hedd. Of course he cared . . . cares . . . about you . . . about Sioned. He's just so . . . feckless. Come on, we'll miss the bus if we don't set out sharpish. I tell you what, if you're both really good, we'll stop at the café and I'll buy you a toasted teacake each.'

So that's it then, I thought. *A whole beautiful school holiday day ruined.*

I trudged up the hill with them towards the bus stop. We don't get many buses coming through each day – so Mam's always in a tiz, even at the best of times, making sure we don't miss the one we want. And the bus goes all round the houses to take you anywhere, so I had plenty of time to wonder about things, to try to work them out, on the journey. I wasn't quite sure what 'feckless' meant but it didn't sound a very nice thing to say about someone. Mam always claims it's rude to call people names. 'Feckless' sounded as if it was name-calling to me. It sounded as if it could be as rude as 'fatso' or 'four-eyes' or 'carrot top'. I looked it up later in the dictionary and I was right too. I think it's wrong when parents say 'don't do this' and 'don't do that' and then go and do the same things themselves. It's not what you'd call fair play, is it? And another thing, why do grown-ups think a toasted teacake is such a treat? It's only hot bread with a couple of squashed-fly currants stuck in it, after all. I mean, it's OK . . . but not exactly exciting. Not as exciting as skateboarding, for example.

It was mid-afternoon by the time we got back. Mam must have felt she'd been rather mean to me by then because she said I could take the skateboard out until tea-time – as long as I stayed on the patch of path where she could see me from the window while she did her ironing. She stood in the doorway and watched while I crossed the road – as if I was still a toddler.

I'd asked for the skateboard for Christmas because I'd wanted to have something – an activity – I could do all by myself. Even I knew I had to get out of my bedroom sometimes and blow the cobwebs away. I didn't want to have to rely on Mam or Dad to take me to a swimming pool or playing field or club, though. Family outings and arrangements always seemed to end in an argument – usually a right slanging match. I didn't want to have to be part of a team either. I didn't want to join in. How could I fit in as part of a crowd when everything about me felt so odd, so out of kilter? I longed to be able to do things alone, in peace, far from any hassle and free from the danger of questions. That's not to say I wanted to appear a complete nerd to anyone who might be passing by. It's pretty tough on your street-cred, I can tell you, when your mam insists on zipping your hoody up for you and seeing you across the road.

'I'm off to surf the pavements,' I called to her over my shoulder. I remembered someone had said that on TV and it sounded the biz. Unfortunately, Mam's a complete wuss and doesn't understand these things. She ruined my effect by giggling.

Luckily the path had dried after the rain. I knew it would've been dangerous to skateboard on a wet surface as the wheels would slip all over the place. My board was a blank with no graphics on the bottom – but I didn't care. I'd put my protective gear on – you know – wristbands and elbow pads. I was still learning back then. I wasn't about to go fast enough to need knee-pads or a helmet.

I stood on the board on the grass first of all – goofy foot forward, regular foot back and shoulder-width apart for balance. I tested what it felt like. I crouched a little and held my arms out from my sides. It felt OK – pretty good, in fact. After a while, I tried kicking the board off along the path. It was safe and smooth with just a slight slope – so I didn't go too fast. Then I took a deep breath, pushed away hard and put my regular foot on the board as well. It was tricky . . . and I wobbled a bit . . . but I didn't have any falls. I was concentrating hard, practising shifting my weight toes-to-heel, heel-to-toes. You have to be able to do that to steer, you see. I had to bail every time I tried a proper turn, though. It was much harder than I'd thought it would be.

'Hello there!'

The voice made me jump. I stepped off the board wrong foot first, tripped over it and sat down on the grass with a bump. I felt a total prat, a real . . . nincompoop, I can tell you.

The green woman stood right behind me. Thankfully, her daughter was nowhere to be seen . . . I'd have gone down in her book as the looniest of loons. I might as well have had LOSER tattooed across my forehead.

'I'm sorry. I didn't intend to startle you. Here, let me help you up.'

'I can manage by myself . . . thanks.'

I knew I had to add the 'thanks' as, even to me, my voice sounded grumpy, sulky and suspicious.

'I . . . I've got to go now. Mam wants me back.'

The green woman followed my gaze as I turned towards our house. Mam waved and beckoned from the bay window.

'You're the boy who was watching us last night, aren't you?'

I nodded.

'I thought I recognized you. Celyn – that's my daughter – and I arrived in town during such a downpour – we were soaked. Two drowned rats. We had a wild splash-about, made the best of it. What a laugh! What a lark! I expect you thought we were quite mad, mad as March hares, dancing about in the rain, didn't you?'

'No . . . not . . .'

'Come on. I'll walk up the road with you. I need to go that way. I've mislaid a puppet. Have you seen him by any chance? An old-fashioned Mr Punch? He's part of my collection and I'd be sad to lose him.'

'I . . . I've got him, actually.'

I don't know why I felt so guilty – but I did.

'Have you now?'

The green woman stared at me. She was one of those people who stand very close to you. Her pearls were pale eyes peeping from the folds of her green clothes. Her own eyes were green, I remember noticing, green flecked with gold. They seemed to be deciphering me, reading my mind. She made me nervous and I found myself starting to babble. It was as if I needed to make excuses for myself, to make excuses for something I hadn't even done.

'We found him on the bench . . . like a gnome . . . top of my wardrobe . . . kept him safe . . . didn't mean . . . didn't really . . . didn't realize he was yours.'

That last bit was a lie, of course. I blushed and scurried off towards home as fast as I could – trying to hide my confusion. I gathered up my board as I went. The green woman kept pace with me, kept close, kept her green eyes fixed on me.

Chapter 3

The green woman and Mam hit it off straight away. Later, when they were best friends, Mam said they got on like a house on fire and that, because they felt the same way about so many things, they were as alike as two peas in a pod. The woman was certainly green enough to be a pea. Later, when he saw them around town, Dad said Mam and her new friend were as thick as thieves. He didn't mean 'thick' as in 'stupid' – although I suppose it's pretty stupid to be a thief. He meant they were always doing things together. Mam said Dad was just green with envy and didn't want her to have any fun without him. Dad said green had always been his least favourite colour . . . and so on, and so on.

I hate it when adults talk to each other in that way. When they to-and-fro, tit-for-tat in those tight, cross voices every time they see each other. It just makes everyone miserable. It wastes time that could be spent doing interesting things, time you could be happy in. It's not as if scoring points off each other even sorts anything out. I think parents are old enough to know better . . . they should be anyhow. If it had been me squabbling, Dad would've banged the table, taken a swipe at me and yelled at me to 'shut up'. Mam would've said 'don't answer back' or 'just do as I say' or sent me up to my room. How come some things are

OK for them to do and not OK for me? Parents eh? I can't figure them out, can you? Completely crazy.

Close up, on that first proper meeting and before we were used to her, the green woman still looked pretty crazy too – extraordinary, in fact. She not only looked extraordinary: we discovered she had the most extraordinary name. It reminded me of the sort of names you find in fairy tales . . . Snow White . . . . Goldilocks . . . Rapunzel . . . . Cinderella . . . one of those ridiculous names that you can't imagine anyone being called in real life. You'll never guess what it was, so I'm going to have to tell you. Wait for it . . . Mistletoe Midwinter. Truly! Ms Mistletoe Midwinter. I ask you! If that's not crazy, what is? Of course, when Dad eventually found out, it gave him the chance to make plenty of jokes and sarcastic comments. I'd had to try hard not to laugh aloud myself when she came out with it. What was even more peculiar was that, when Mam used to notice that I was sad, she never asked why I was depressed or glum or in the doldrums or blue . . . or . . . whatever. She never used any of those common expressions to describe being miserable. Instead, she always lifted my chin and smiled at me very gently and said, 'Why the mid-winters?'

Back then, it really used to get to me when she did that. I'd think: *As if she doesn't know.*

Anyway, I could tell even Mam was rather startled initially when that strange green woman arrived with me at our front door, claimed to be the owner of Punch and introduced herself. Mam had blinked hard, but managed to stay calm and keep a straight face, as she shook hands.

'Nice to meet you. I'm so glad we've solved the puppet mystery so quickly and easily . . . um . . . M . . . Mistletoe.'

'I know, I know.'

The green woman smiled as Mam stumbled over her name, and our hallway lit up as if the sun had just come out from behind a cloud and sparkled across snow, across ice.

'I was born at midwinter, you see, and my surname was Midwinter – so I suppose my parents thought 'Mistletoe' would be especially suitable. Parents eh?'

Mistletoe winked at me. It wasn't an awful wink – like Punch's had been. It was friendly and jolly, a sudden flicker of brightness linking us together.

'I must admit, it can be a bit of a burden at times. My own daughter was born at midwinter too – so, somehow, I felt I had to follow family tradition. I hope Celyn finds her name easier to live with than mine though. I tell you what, call me Mitzi – lots of people do.

'Right,' said Mam. 'How lovely.'

I could tell she found 'Mitzi' almost as hard to take as 'Mistletoe' and to me it was even worse – as if it disguised who she really was – you know, like an alias.

'Come on in. I'll make some tea and Hedd can find Mr Punch for you.'

I remember the way Mistletoe Midwinter bent towards me. I remember the way her eyes held mine.

It wasn't as if she did anything out of the ordinary, only that the effect she had wasn't normal. I sensed she was different. There were her weird clothes and her batty name, of course, but there was also a force in her, some sort of . . . power. It showed itself in those sun-spangled, melt-water green eyes, in that spring-day-coming smile. It made me very uncomfortable. It was as if her eyes lit up my mind and then read it like a book. I felt she could decode my past, predict my future. It terrified me. I dragged my eyes away from hers and scowled at the floor.

'Hedd . . .' Mistletoe considered my name, held it as one long syllable on her tongue. Then she turned to Mam and laughed.

'He certainly doesn't appear very peaceful, more . . . belligerent, bellicose, pugnacious!'

Mam flushed and interrupted hurriedly.

'Well . . . he's not really quite himself. He's been rather upset since . . .'

For one dreadful moment I'd thought Mam was going to tell this strange woman all about our lives. Hold her hair back and show that fading bruise just above her cheekbone. Explain how my dad had gone . . . and why Mam had finally kicked him out.

'. . . since . . . Christmas.' Mam finished her sentence.

I unclenched my teeth, my fists. The palms of my hands were sweating. I hate it when parents tell other adults things about you when you're standing right there in front of them. The words fly between them over your head – as if you don't even exist, as if you're nobody, as if you're nothing. As if – oh no – you couldn't possibly be old enough or sensible enough or important enough to speak up for yourself. And they've usually got things all round the twist. It's so rude, isn't it? And I bet they wouldn't want it done to them either. I didn't understand 'belligerent' or 'bellicose' or 'pugnacious' and that made me cross. I looked them up later and I supposed Mistletoe thought of all those fighting words because my hands had been curled tight into fists. *Ha! You were wrong there, clever clogs,* I'd thought as I closed the dictionary with a snap. *It was nervousness . . . fear . . . that caused my scowl, my clenched fists.*

Sioned had taken hold of Mistletoe's flowing skirt and tugged her towards the kitchen behind Mam. Sioned's usually rather shy and wary of new people but she was as happy as a pig in muck with Mistletoe straight away. I went upstairs, stood on a chair, and yanked Punch down from the wardrobe.

Mistletoe was delighted to have Mr Punch back again. She stroked his tufty hair – just as Dad used to stroke mine when I was little. Before everything got so angry. Before everything exploded . . . fell apart.

'He's very old, you see, and really quite valuable. I've had him such a long time that I couldn't bear to think he'd gone forever. Even when you told me you'd found him, I was worried he might've been damaged by the rain. I was so cross with Celyn for getting him out of the bag at all. I don't know what she could've been thinking of. And then she goes and forgets where she's put him. She'd lose her own head if it wasn't screwed on to her shoulders, that girl. She's a real day dreamer . . . although sometimes there's method in her madness. Oh . . . yes please . . . I'll have a quick cup of tea but I can't stop long. We've rented a house along the front, beyond the harbour. I've left Celyn indoors waiting for the removal van to arrive with all our other belongings. We only brought our overnight bags and a few essentials with us yesterday evening – and precious Punch, of course.'

I could tell Mistletoe was going to be one of those women who can talk the hind legs off a donkey. I'd always thought that, if they gave an eisteddfod chair for chatter, then my mam would win it every time – no probs – but Mistletoe Midwinter could certainly give her a run for her money. I'd felt rather bad when I thought of the way I'd bumped Mr Punch up the stairs. The way his precious head had taken thump after thump. The way I'd swung him by one ancient arm and flung him across the room, then that dull thud as he'd hit the top of the wardrobe and the way he'd crumpled up into the corner like . . . well . . . like a puppet really. How come I'd hated and feared him so much? As I said, he seemed quite different in that morning's light. Sort of sad, pitiful-old instead of creepy-and-cantankerous-old. It throws you when things change overnight, doesn't it? It's kind of muddling when you feel completely different from one day to the next. When that happened back then, it used to make me anxious – sort of permanently on edge. Sometimes it was as if I couldn't trust anything . . . or anybody any more.

I'd glanced sideways at Mr Punch's painted face,

hoping it wasn't chipped or scraped. Luckily he seemed OK . . . although he'd picked up a coating of dust from the top of my wardrobe. Mam says life's too short to waste it doing jobs like dusting, that only need doing all over again in the blink of an eye, before you can say Jack Robinson. Mam says people who want their surfaces to be fit for a queen to eat her dinner off, can shake their tail feathers and do their own dusting.

Mistletoe brushed the cobwebs from Punch with her sleeve and beamed at him.

'He's a very . . . unusual item to be carrying around,' Mam said in her most polite voice.

She gave me one of her warning glances, so I knew she didn't want me to open my mouth and make comments about him being ugly enough to give people nightmares. Adults are fond of meaningful looks, aren't they? You're supposed to work out what they're saying without them speaking. I think it's really unreasonable. Our teacher, Mr Phillips, has a stare that says 'stop fidgeting' or 'don't talk to the person next to you when I'm talking' or 'don't interrupt'. It's the same stare for all those things but I understand that now. I know that we just have to let him go droning on and on and listen quietly until he eventually decides to stop. Then, if we're good and with any luck, that might be before the mountains wear down to the sea and the rivers all run dry.

Sometimes adults use their looks on other adults too. 'I'm trying to catch her eye,' Mam always says, putting on a bright, querying expression when Sioned's fussing in a café and the waitress is ignoring us and we're all starving and have already been sat there since doomsday. The waitress never takes any notice of Mam's face and so she always has to wave her hand about as well or hoist Sioned on her hip and struggle over the push-chair to the counter.

Dad could flash a face that was the fiercest I've ever seen. An if-looks-could-kill glare. He never used it outside our house, though. Often, it flicked on and off so fast that it was tricky to be sure of it – before it was too late. I used to be exhausted, watching all the time, waiting, hardly daring to breathe in case I conjured it up. It was so difficult to keep my wits about me . . . keep one jump ahead . . . avoid trouble. Even if everything seemed OK and Dad was jolly, I always knew that fearsome face lurked inside him somewhere. It made me twitchy – as if we were all walking a tightrope and might fall off at any minute. Mam said being in the same house as Dad was like walking on egg shells and that was about right too. Even Mam found it hard to judge when Dad's face, Dad's mood, might suddenly change. Dad said she wound him up. Dad said Mam didn't know when to stop. Sometimes – now and then – I saw it coming before she did.

The next few days plodded past – deadly slow. Slower than a tortoise, slower than a snail, slower even than a slow boat to China. We saw nothing of Mistletoe and Celyn and I supposed they were busy unpacking.

To me, the whole world seemed shuttered, closed

down, confined to a fogged, cold and sodden gloaming. It was like being Jonah, swallowed up and all alone inside a whale. It was a nothing time, a nowhere place. I thought a lot about that saying, you know the one I mean, about the darkest time being just before the dawn. It went round and round inside my head. I was certainly surrounded by darkness but I couldn't imagine, in those bleak days, the slightest hint or hope of dawn. Crows circled the chimney pots. I lay on my bed and listened to them crying, watched as they wheeled like blown cinders past my window.

'For goodness sake, go out and play,' Mam said. 'You're no good to man nor beast drooping about the house. You're doing my head in. Go on – skedaddle!'

So I took my board and practised on the tarmac in that empty little strip of park high above the sea. No one came to sit on the benches at that season, not even Mr Punch, and only grumpy dog-walkers hurried through, heads down and scowling as I got to grips with carving in between them. I was determined to master those basic turns. I kept my feet over the trucks – you know, those metal pieces that hold the wheels on – bent my knees and did the whole heel-to-toes, toes-to-heel weight-shifting bit that everyone tells you will work. I wanted my carving to be fluid – like you see in films when someone's surfing or snowboarding. I wanted to feel that free. I wanted to fly. I tried to keep all my movements smooth and to make a snaky 'S' shape down the path. I tried and tried again. I was improving. I was getting there. Practice makes perfect, as they say. I learnt to tilt the deck in the direction I wanted to go, to tighten my turns by leaning into them. Gradually, I cracked it. Back and forth I meandered, back and forth across the incline of the path.

I never went down to the square by the chip shop where all the other children skated. I knew that the low walls around the Tourist Information Centre are excellent for jumps and that the others had put together a make-shift ramp too – but Mam always wanted me to be where she could keep an eye on me, check I was all right.

A bit late for that, isn't it? I thought. *How can anyone be all right when the whole world as they know it's come to an end? How can I be OK when I'm living in my own worst nightmare? I know . . . I know . . . Dad's a walking nightmare when he's with us . . . but he is my dad after all. Thinking about him is too hard. It makes my head ache. Why couldn't the two of you be bothered to make more effort, if not for yourselves then for Sioned . . . or for me . . . And you're always telling me to look on the bright side – but I can't find the smallest glimmer of a bright side to even peep at. Why couldn't we be a happy family, the same as those you see in adverts on TV – the ones where it's sunshine all the way, a picture perfect paradise?*

Luckily, Sioned was too small to brood all the time as I did but, like Mam, she also wanted to keep me close, as if I might disappear once she'd let me out of her sight. Sioned liked to stand on a chair if I was skateboarding and watch me from the window. To Sioned, I was the best skateboarder ever – a champion – even though I was still a beginner. She'd clap and clap and cheer me on. I'm so much older than Sioned that, to her, I'm a hero – just as my dad used to be to me. Little kids . . . they don't know any better, do they? Things seem so easy, so straightforward, when you're that young but . . . you don't know you're born.

I didn't really want to skate with anyone else, even if Mam had let me go – you know, untied me from her apron strings. I couldn't bear to have to laugh and joke and smile one of those false smiles – a cheesy grin, like a mask – all the time. I certainly didn't want to answer any questions. There was another reason too. If I'd joined in those games on the square, I'd have been near Dad as he pottered about, patching and polishing his boat for the tourists. Once I'd loved helping him – but everything had become different and difficult between us. Still . . . I knew that, if he saw me, Dad would've come over to chat as if everything was the same as before, as if nothing at all had happened or changed. Even worse, I might've had to put up with smirks and nudges from the others as he wove his way, so stumbling and so scruffy, between the boat and pub and back again . . . embarrassing or what? Mam said Dad was going to seed – as if he were some old hollyhock. Mam said Dad was making an exhibition of himself. Mam said Dad was a dead loss and we were all better off without him. Some of what she said was fair enough, all things considered. I still missed him though – my old dad, my dim and distant dad, my OK dad, I mean.

Mam talked about Dad a lot – and most of it was uncomplimentary. I suppose Sioned was too young to talk to, but Mam would go over and over everything with me. I didn't want to know. Well . . . what I'm saying is, I did already know but I didn't see the sense in going on and on about it.

What happened to 'least said, soonest mended'? I'd thought.

Parents always want to talk things through, don't they? I had no interest in discussions. I just wanted it all to vanish or, preferably, to never have occurred in the first place. I wanted to turn the clock back – way, way back. Mam went on complaining about Dad – even though I never answered her and she might as well've been talking to the wall. When she moaned, her voice changed into that whine that used to wind Dad up something rotten. Sometimes, when they argued, Dad used to say:

'Don't start!'

and then . . .

'Give it a rest!'

and then . . .

'You don't know when to stop!'

and then . . .

ZAP   POW   BANG

Home would blow up in front of my eyes like a scene in a comic strip and . . . that would be the end of Mam's point of view.

If I could see it coming, I'd push my way between them and yell at Dad and yell at Mam to stop. But

Mam is one of those people who must have the last word. She would just plough on regardless and then Dad would suddenly snap, lose the plot completely, and transform in a flash into his other self – a Mr Punch-ing caricature of a man, the nastiest of cartoon nasties, a horror movie. Then –

ZAP POW BANG

– and that would be me shut up, that would be me stopped in my tracks, that would be me shown what's what and taught a lesson to remember.

Is it any wonder that I wasn't keen on talking? Words can be wonderful. I love words. But, make no mistake, words can be dangerous too, lead you into trouble. Words are more powerful than people think. Words can trick and taunt, words can hurt and harm – words aren't always a good thing, in my experience. I've usually got a favourite word of the moment, though, haven't you? My top-of-the-chart, best word in the universe back then was – abracadabra. That's a mysterious word and the sound of it is fantastic on your tongue – it has a rhythm like a tap dance. I used to wish I could say: 'Abracadabra!' to change all our pasts.

I used to wish I could say: 'Abracadabra!' and alter all our futures.

About a week after we'd returned the puppet to her, Mistletoe sent a note inviting us all to a 'house-warming tea' at four o'clock on Saturday afternoon.

'I've never had an invitation to afternoon tea before,' said Mam. 'How posh!'

'It might be more like a toddlers' tea party than anything fancy,' I said. 'They happen in the afternoon as well – but I can't say I've seen or heard of a toddler belonging to Mistletoe and Celyn. Perhaps it'll be similar to the Mad Hatter's tea party in Alice in Wonderland . . .'

I was, despite myself, very intrigued. Mistletoe was a puzzle. Mistletoe was full of a peculiar energy that I couldn't fathom. It made me nervous but it wasn't the same sort of nervous Dad used to make me feel. It was unsettling – gave me a fluttering in my stomach, a tingling down my spine. Her power was oddly awesome – but it attracted me too. I imagined that a Midwinter tea party might prove to be very unusual.

Sioned grabbed at the note. It was leaf-shaped, shiny and shaded in soft greens with spiky writing in darker green ink. Two beads, one holly berry red and one as opalescent as mistletoe fruit, were looped through a hole at the end of the invitation on a narrow, bronze ribbon. It was a very exotic communication. We don't often get proper letters in our house. Most people telephone or e-mail or text when they want to contact each other. Our post is really boring – mostly adverts or dull envelopes with those see-through windows to show the address. Our post used to depress Dad.

'Bills and more bills,' he'd say, chucking them in the bin unopened. 'What do they expect . . . blood out of a stone?'

We'd never had a note like the one from Mistletoe and Celyn either. The only notes I'd seen before had been quick and practical – written on torn scraps of paper or on a lined page ripped from a cheap writing pad. Even the grandest Christmas or birthday cards had never appeared as lovely and as luscious as the Midwinters' invitation did. It certainly wasn't the sort of summons you wanted to refuse.

'Oh no you don't! I know it looks good enough to eat but, if you put it in your mouth, you'll make it soggy and spoilt – not to mention probably choking on those beads.'

Mam whipped the tantalizing leaflet out of Sioned's reach and propped it up on top of the TV. It glinted – tempting as all the pick 'n' mix in Woolworth. I could understand Sioned thinking it was edible.

Suddenly, I could hardly wait for Saturday to come.

However it turns out, I thought, *at least, after all the miserable times we've had and after such an awful Christmas, we'll have had this pleasure of . . . of something new to look forward to . . .*

It's funny, isn't it? A mid-winter tea party with people we hardly knew – it doesn't sound much at all – even now. But that tea party started something. That simple tea party brought a breath of fresh air, a wind of change.

Chapter 4

The Midwinters were renting one of the terraced houses on the opposite side of the bay to us. We look down on the lifeboat station, a crescent of sand, the harbour with its jingle and jostle of boats and the wide curve of the harbour wall. On the days when Dad and I used to work on his boat, we'd always have a walk together along the harbour wall before returning home. There's an upper and lower level you can walk along and steep stone steps joining the two. On the wall of the lower level there are huge iron rings, aged and rusty, for mooring boats and, when you're young, you have to be careful not to trip over the ropes and chains that sometimes criss-cross the walkway. Dad would look after me, keep me safe and far away from the edge. Mam had it wrong, you see, when she said he didn't take care of me, watch out for me. He didn't worry about things that bothered Mam – such as keeping my clothes clean or remembering to get us both home at the proper time for tea . . . and stuff like that. When I was little, though, he seemed to know everything there was to know, to be able to protect me from all harm or unhappiness.

The upper level is the best to walk along. Sometimes we'd get an ice-cream first and it would make Mam mad when she found out . . . because that's spoiling your appetite and filling yourself up with junk instead of food that's good for you – spinach and beetroot and swede and such. Dad and I both love ice cream, so often we'd still have one anyway and stroll along hand in hand enjoying them. It's funny, when you're a kid, you don't mind holding hands with people, do you? Sometimes our teacher still tries to get us to hold hands with a partner in P.E. or if we've got to walk somewhere on a class outing and we all think that's the absolute end. Or Mam tries to hold my hand around the shops – when I'm twelve now for crying out loud. How wet can you get? Do I look like the sort of dummy who would get himself lost? It's fine holding hands with Sioned, of course, partly because she is the sort of Dumbo who'd get lost, and with Dad on those evenings on the harbour wall it was OK too. It was more than OK, in fact . . . kind of . . . warm and cosy. The houses of the town clustered close behind us, rose in tiers up the hillsides, their ice cream colours – strawberry, mocha, pistachio, vanilla, blackcurrant, fudge – glowing melt-in-your-mouth in the early evening sunshine.

If we were in luck, the dolphins would be swimming in the cove on the far side of the wall and Dad would lift me up onto the high parapet and clutch me close while we watched them play. Our dolphins are famous. They're nosy too and often follow the tourist boats, leaping the wake while all the holiday-makers twist and turn in their seats, tracking the sheen and gleam of arced dolphin backs with cameras.

When we'd arrived right at the end of the harbour wall, we'd sit for a while. We'd look north towards the mountains and Dad promised to take me there some day.

'We'll climb the highest peak in the land together,' he said, 'just the two of us. There we'll be – on top of the world – you and me, kings of the castle, lords of all we survey.'

We'd lick our ice creams in silence for a bit and I'd nibble the pointy base from my cornet so I always got drips and dribbles down my T-shirt. We'd gaze out towards the horizon where boats disappeared between the sea and sky as if our bay were a brimming bowl and they had sailed right up to the rim and plunged over into the unknown, into nothing.

Then Dad would wipe our fingers and my face on his handkerchief and tell me stories of fabulous sea creatures – mer-people, seal women, water horses, tales of drowned cities, legends of magical islands. He could chronicle pilgrimages, all those coracled crossings of saints, and replay the whole history of our town. He'd learned about the bustle of our bay in the days when it was a busy port, had studied books from the library, could recite the old lists of wares transported in and out of our little haven. The boards recording custom dues can still be found nailed up between the harbour wall and the town. I love to read them now but Dad knew them by heart – weights, prices, goods. The words are rare and rhythmic as a poem. In Dad's voice, chanted against the evening song of seagulls, they became even more special. Slow and deep as a tolled bell, they rolled from Dad's tongue . . . like some incantation against bad luck, like a charm to hold the moment, like a prayer:

Chests, crates, casks,
flasks, bundles, bushels,
barrels, butts, baskets,
puncheons and hundredweights.
Guineas, crowns, shillings,
halfpennies and farthings.
Middlings, culm, ivory,
unwrought iron, oysters,
molasses, lime, indigo,
taffeta and barleymead.

Sailors and seamstresses, maidservants and merchants, farmers and fishermen, peers and poets – all the people of the past stirred into life around the bay as my dad talked into the dusk. My favourite story, the one he always saved until last, was about the old pepper-pot-shaped lighthouse that once stood 'right in the very spot we're sitting now', as he always said, and which was washed away long ago in a single night of terrible storm. We always went home after that story, and Mam was always crotchety because we were late and I was grubby, but Dad could always cheer her up, raise her smile, make her laugh out loud. Those days are always wonderful in my memory, and always, always sunny. My dad was the best dad possible and always fine and strong. I was always so proud of him, he always kept his promises and his stories were always true. I believed that fairy tale time would never change – that I'd always feel that secure, that sure, that loved – always and forever.

'Forever is a long time' is a sad saying and people

say it in such a sad tone of voice. What they really mean is 'dream on' and 'you must be joking' and 'no way'. And they're right, of course. I know that now. My early childhood seems like a dream, a myth, a never-never land.

The Midwinters' new home looked down over the small cove on the far side of our harbour wall – the same cove where Dad and I used to watch the dolphins swimming.

Don't start thinking about Dad. Not now. Don't go upsetting yourself.

That's what adults say, isn't it? As if the upset were somehow your own fault and nothing to do with them at all. I hung back behind Mam and Sioned to collect myself. That's another thing grown-ups say – as if you've been broken into bits and have to gather up the scattered pieces and fit them all back into place to be whole again. What I want to know is – how can you be expected to do that by yourself, if you're all smashed to smithereens?

I pretended to be enjoying the view. Beyond the harbour and the town was the sprawl of the caravan park and then, way in the distance, the mountains of Snowdonia curved around Cardigan Bay – a dragon tail, a fortification, a question mark.

Questions, always questions, I thought. *It's as if my head's stuffed with as many question marks as feathers in a cushion. Why? What if? Shouldn't they have? Couldn't I have? What on earth happens next? Where do we go from here? Questions squiggling through my brain – day in, day* out – tangled as tadpoles in a pond. *Questions, stupid questions . . . but never any answers.*

'Ask me no questions and I'll tell you no lies,' Mam said to me once when she was in a particularly bad mood.

But it hurts, doesn't it, when you're bursting with questions that won't go away? Questions weigh you down, rest heavy as a great bluestone on your chest. Questions stopper your breath, bubble in your throat until you think you'll choke. Questions make you ache and make you want to scream when they're bottled up inside you.

'Put a sock in it. Keep a lid on it. Pull yourself together,' I muttered to myself.

The mountains were sharp green that day, shimmering in a spill of winter sunshine but, like the sea, our mountains are always changing: to different greens, to blue, to indigo, to black. Sometimes they're capped in cloud, sometimes shawled in snow. Often, they disappear altogether, vanish behind rain or are lost in mist. I shook myself. It was a good outlook for the Midwinters to have, varied and variable – and better than . . . than a view of a brick wall, for example.

Some changes are interesting, aren't they? Lots of people claim change keeps you fresh, keeps you on your toes, keeps you alive.

'A change is as good as a rest,' they say.

It's a puzzle to work out what's for the best, really, who's telling the truth. I hate it when you have to make your mind up. I hate it when you have to take sides. Why does everything have to get so muddled and complicated? It drives you potty, ties you up in knots. As I stood in that lane above the bay, heading for the tea-party, I suddenly wanted stillness and strength and . . . certainty. I wanted a port in a storm and a safe harbour. I wanted peace. Our family had been shipwrecked and I wanted a great solid chunk of rock to cling to.

I thought about Enlli anchored out there, static among the swirling seas, at the very edge of sight. Enlli . . . the mystical island of saints from Dad's stories. Dad claims Merlin bides his time there, still watches over our bay, century after century after century. His magical chamber of glass still clings, invisible, to the sea cliffs. It cheered me up imagining old Merlin dwelling in his vast, crystal limpet – always on the look out. How long do you think his beard would be by now? Longer than a country mile? Longer than all the lanes in Wales linked together, I reckon. I bet he's wrapped himself up in it, sits cocooned in a downy duvet of hair. A glass home's like a conservatory, after all – and they get pretty chilly in the winter. Even the Enlli lighthouse hasn't been swept away in a storm as ours has. It still strokes the sea with wide arcs of light – warning, guiding, guarding, safe keeping.

'We'll go to Enlli together,' Dad used to say, 'just you and me. We'll sail those stormy straits and reach that stronghold. We'll be safe and snug as a pair of saints – except my boat will be much more comfy than a coracle.'

Dad was full of promises.

I intend to visit Enlli one day, even if I have to go all

by myself. I made my mind up, there and then, on that very afternoon, the minute the island swam into my mind. It's now an ambition of mine. It's good to have ambitions, isn't it? They make you look forward to the future instead of back to the past. Ambitions are hopeful and regrets . . . are . . . just sad.

Trust the Midwinters to pick a house with a magical view, I thought. *Mistletoe's probably signalling to Merlin across the sea from her window at this very moment. Merlin's a wizard, after all, and Mistletoe seems pretty witch-like herself to me.*

I turned around. Mam and Sioned were waiting for me at the Midwinters' front door.

'Buck up!' Mam called. 'Stop dilly-dallying! Stop shilly-shallying!'

What're they like, parents? Do they try to embarrass you on purpose?

A scarlet curtain moved in an upstairs window . . . but no one's face appeared.

I waited as a lorry rattled past from the whelk-packing station. Have you ever smelt the whiff of whelks on the wind? Mam says they're pungent. In other words – they simply stink. Then I hurried across to Mam and Sioned – still holding my nose.

The inside of the Midwinter house was amazing. It was as colourful as a fairground – a riot of brightly painted furniture, rainbow cushions. Surfaces over-flowed with fascinating knick-knacks that made you itch to touch them. They glowed and glistened – as tempting and brilliant as Christmas baubles. It was startling, stupendous. It made my head spin. Just walking into the Midwinter house banished winter's bare branches, barren fields, bleak weather – in spite of the name. Their home buzzed with brightness, hummed with contentment – so that the cold cries of crows faded, became distant and unimportant. It was like stepping inside a spinning kaleidoscope. It was a hurdy-gurdy, hunky-dory, hullabaloo of a house. I was speechless. Even Sioned was gaping – silenced for once, gripping Mam's hand and gobsmacked as a goldfish.

Puppets were everywhere – and I mean everywhere. Puppets dangled and danced from the ceiling, hung from each curtain rail. Finger puppets peeped from eggcups on the dresser. Hand puppets perched on side-tables, on chair backs, on bookshelves – mobbed the mantelpiece. There were puppets on strings and puppets on sticks. There were tiny puppets and tall puppets. There was a papier mâché pirate, a wooden crocodile with a great, gnashy grin. There were puppets made of cloth, cut from card, coiled on springs. There were plastic puppets, paper bag puppets, ancient puppets and still-in-their-box brand new puppets. There were oh-so-pretty princess puppets, gaudy in their gauzy gowns. There were dragons and dinosaurs, goblins and ghosts. There were happy and sad puppets, ornate puppets and plain puppets. Everywhere I looked, puppet arms and legs tangled, lolled and swung as if they were alive. There was a huge table in the centre of the room heaped with sewing things and several half-made puppets. In the middle of them all, in pride of place – proud as punch, you might say – sat Mr Punch. Ruddy-cheeked, hook-nosed, hunch-backed, he called out to me. I knew I wasn't imagining it. I knew I wasn't dreaming. That time, he really and truly did call my name.

'He-edd! He-edd!'

His voice was grating – part groan, part cackle.

Sioned squealed and clutched at Mam.

'For goodness sake, Celyn, you'll frighten everyone to death,' said Mistletoe as she ushered us all into the room in front of her.

Celyn stood up. I'd not noticed her sitting low on a footstool behind Mr Punch. I'd been too busy studying everything else in the room and her green clothes, so stunning in the street, didn't stand out as extra-ordinary in the vivid surroundings of her home.

'Sorry,' she said. 'It was only meant as a joke. Look . . .' She put an arm around Sioned and showed her a sort of metal lozenge she had in her hand. 'It's a swozzle. You suck on it as you speak and it makes the puppet's scratchy voice.'

'Swozzle' is a strange word. I'd heard of 'swizzle' but I'd never come across 'swozzle' before. Some words get used all the time, don't they? Some words get used so much they become boring and all the glory seems to drain out of them. 'Swozzle' hardly gets used at all. Rare words are special, I think. They make you sit up and take notice.

Mam and Sioned and I all tried to speak in Punch's voice using the swozzle but none of us could get it right.

'It's a knack,' laughed Mistletoe. 'Sit yourselves down and I'll bring in the tea things.'

We wedged ourselves into bungey, pillowy chairs –

each clearing a small space between the bits and bobs, the oddments, the all sorts. Puppet wigs tickled our necks, puppet elbows nudged our knees and puppet toes tweaked our sides. I scooped a puppet skeleton out of the way and re-arranged a cushion to protect me from the hard point of a fox-puppet's snout. The crocodile's snappy teeth were dangerously close to my left ear but, by then, I was too hungry to worry.

Afternoon tea came on trays – as if we were at a fete, a garden party or a picnic. Everything Mistletoe offered up was bite-sized and each different mouthful was perfectly delicious. I ate:

two spicy samosas
one mushroomy tartlet
five small sausages dipped in honey
two cherry tomatoes
a handful of nuts
three itsy-bitsy pizza pieces (salami – my favourite)
a morsel of cheese
one mini pitta pocket (filled with risotto
and hard to get into my mouth all in one go
although I did my best
so that Mam said: 'Hedd, really!'
in that disappointed tone parents have
when you've let them down
and shown them up
but I still couldn't say 'sorry'
because that would have been
eating-with-my-mouth-full
and, anyway, I wanted to gobble up

the next yummy tit-bits)
two miniscule onion bhajis
one skewer of chicken satay
four chunks of crispy raw vegetables
(two carrot, two celery)
six scrumptious orange segments dipped in chocolate
three swirly-curly almond biscuits
one cute, pastel pink fairy-cake
with an iced flower on top.

I would have had extra fairy-cakes if they hadn't been so girly looking. Sioned ate more fairy-cakes than any thing else and surrounded herself with a crumb mountain but no one else seemed to notice – let alone mind. Nobody protested even when she picked all the icing-sugar flowers off the left-over cakes. She planted them in a neat row along the edge of her tray and sang a song under her breath.

'Mary, Mary, quite contrary,

How does your garden grow?'

It's amazing Mam's got the nerve to ever criticize my table manners when we've got oink-oink piggy Sioned to deal with.

Mam and Mistletoe were talking nineteen to the dozen, as if they'd been best friends for years. I heard Mam say she'd love to have a go at making puppets. I heard Mam say she'd always wanted to do something different, something out-of-the-ordinary, something creative – which was news to me. I stretched out my legs. I was feeling rather puffed after so much food. I glanced across the room and caught Celyn's eye.

Chapter 5

'C'mon,' said Celyn. 'Let's go and play upstairs.'

'Good idea,' said Mistletoe. 'You can all go off and leave us women to have a natter, get to know each other better. More tea?' she asked Mam. 'I've quite a selection here, so you can have a change from raspberry. Take your pick: peppermint, cranberry, camomile, orange blossom, apple and cinnamon ...'

Mam and Mistletoe bent their heads together, stirred the bright sachets of fruits and herbs. Mistletoe was very charming and Mam already seemed to have fallen under her spell. I watched them. They suddenly appeared different . . . wise women, wicca, witches . . . a sorceress and her apprentice . . . fingering tisanes and tinctures, potions and poisons . . . brewing up . . . who knew what? I shook my head to get rid of the image. I'd given the strange infusions a miss myself and stuck to home-made lemonade. Dad and I like proper tea, big warming mugs of PG Tips.

Celyn took Sioned's hand and I followed them upstairs. Celyn had a room with stars on the ceiling and holly prints stencilled around the walls.

'Mistletoe always does them for me,' she explained as she noticed me staring. 'My room's immediately decorated with holly as soon as we arrive somewhere new. We move around so much, you see – never stay long in one place – but the holly comes with us, turns anywhere into home.'

'Deck the halls with boughs of holly . . .' I sang – then felt a fool. Why do I always open my big mouth and say – or, even more toe-curling, sing – the first thing that comes into my head? Celyn either failed to notice, or kindly chose to ignore, my discomfort.

'That's it,' she said calmly. 'Mistletoe's got her own print too. It's lovely – bunches of greeny-gold leaves with splashes of silvery berries. A real frosted, midwinter frieze of mistletoe.'

Fortunately, I couldn't immediately think of a song about mistletoe – so managed, for once, to hold my tongue and keep my foot out of my mouth.

There were more puppets in Celyn's room and an old-fashioned puppet theatre stood in one corner.

'We give puppet shows,' said Celyn, 'on the beaches in the summer time, or at fetes, festivals and fairs. We travel far and wide, go everywhere and anywhere. We're the Midwinter nomads.'

I thought of the Punch and Judy shows I'd sometimes seen. The shouting and arguing between the puppet characters, the bashing and beating and 'that's-the-way-to-do-it' as Punch lashed out with his stick. The memory haunted me, made me shudder.

'Not traditional Punch and Judy shows,' Celyn continued, as if she knew what was in my mind. 'Mistletoe collects old puppets as a hobby, out of interest, but we don't do those kind of shows. Our performances are filled with original puppets that Mistletoe and I have made and contain stories from fairy tales, from legends, and from our own imaginations. And sometimes we throw in tricks and juggling, somersaults and stilt-walking. I tell you what, we can make up a show together now and that'll give you an idea of how it works.'

So Celyn, Sioned and I played at performing a puppet show. I had a girl-puppet on strings. Her limbs seemed to have a life of their own and were hard to control properly. She had yellow plaits that curled up like bananas on each side of her face and painted-on freckles and the soppiest smile you've ever seen. I think Celyn must've been having a laugh when she picked that one for me. She had a different type of puppet, one that cavorted crazily on sticks and could be tumbled and twisted to imitate the clumsiest of clowns. We used hand puppets too and, both together, made a paper dragon prowl and coil and fly in rippled waves of movement. Sioned sat on the edge of the bed as an audience – clapping and laughing and calling for more. Sometimes she joined in with a set of finger puppets, five different little characters – a king, a cat, a pixie, an owl, an old woman. They scuttled and shuffled across the stage – one by one or in a cluttered handful – and didn't do or say too much because Sioned couldn't manage it. She enjoyed playing, even though her puppets kept slipping from her fingers. We both had a good time. It was fun. I realized that I hadn't seen Sioned as full of beans for ages. Celyn's game lifted a weight from our shoulders, helped us to forget for a while. I felt . . . well, it's hard to explain . . . just like . . . just like an everyday child again, I suppose.

Celyn was a great puppeteer. She could manage all sorts of different voices and really brought her puppets to life in the way she made them move. After a while, she tried to teach me how to juggle with just two soft, leather balls. I was hopeless – a complete ding-bat. I kept dropping the balls or hitting myself or the lampshade or the furniture with them. One even landed right on Sioned's head. I couldn't keep two balls in the air at the same time – never mind any more. Celyn kept trying to show me how it was done.

'Just start with one ball and throw it from hand to hand at different heights,' she said.

'Focus your eyes at the top of the ball's arc,' she said.

'Let the balls fly through your field of vision, don't watch them,' she said.

'Keep your palms facing up, keep your wrists relaxed,' she said.

'Try kneeling on the floor. It'll stop you moving forward as you juggle,' she said.

Eventually I gave up.

'You're brilliant,' I said, as Celyn spun several balls at speed in a complex pattern. She tossed one up behind her back and caught it in her other hand. She lobbed balls under her knees and didn't drop a single one. The balls revolved so fast, it was hard to keep track of them.

'You're brill! You're brill!' shouted Sioned, bouncing up and down on the bed for all she was worth. She was beside herself, carried away, completely . . . carefree. Little kids – honestly – they can get so over-excited.

Celyn caught the balls. We sat down on the bed beside Sioned to calm her down before she bounced into the end of next week.

'I could never do that,' I told Celyn.

'It's only practice. I've been doing it for years and years – ever since I can remember. Anyway, I can't skateboard at all and I'd love to do that. I've seen you practising every day this week – getting better and better.'

I got that hot feeling that comes when your face is turning bright red and there's nothing you can do to stop it . . . and thinking about it only makes things worse. I realized Celyn could see right across the bay, right across the harbour to the path where I attempted my basic skateboard moves. Our house and the Midwinter house directly faced each other, across the water, across the town. It was as if the Midwinters had come especially to observe us, to keep an eye on us, watch over us.

'Why don't you skateboard with the others,' said Celyn, 'the ones who meet on the square? Don't you know them? Aren't they your friends?'

'They are and they aren't,' I muttered. It sounded a mad, a stupid answer – even to myself.

Why should I tell you anything? Mind your own business, Ms Nosy Parker. I thought but, somehow, I still found myself trying to explain.

Celyn and Mistletoe both had that effect on you. You'd wonder at their extraordinary otherness and then trust them completely with . . . with anything, with everything, really.

Of course I knew those other children. I'd always known them – been to toddler group with them, been all through primary school with them and I knew I'd be starting at the comp with them that coming September. We'd been in and out of each other's houses for most of our lives. They knew me well . . . too well. They were too close for comfort – knew more about me, and my family, than I wanted them to know. I was fed up with all that poking and prying and . . . pitying. Everyone knows everyone around here. It's a small world. Everyone knows everything about everyone – right down to your second cousin twice removed and what you had for breakfast a fortnight ago. It used to make me feel fixed, you know, pinned down and set in stone. It was as if nothing and nobody could ever change – and you just had to put up with it.

I told Celyn how I felt. It was a relief, in a funny sort of way, to let someone else know. I didn't mention that Mam also wanted to keep me close to her, make me super-safe as if that would wipe out the past. I'd have sounded so pathetic, a right Mummy's boy. I'd intended to just say that I preferred being on my own, that I wasn't at all lonely and liked my own company. But Celyn shook back her bob of bright hair and it startled me. She cuddled Sioned close and fixed me with her sharp, green eyes and a smile as wide as the whole world – and the words just tumbled out, all different.

'It would be easier . . . better . . . to have someone . . . a friend . . . I don't know so well. One who's a bit . . . different and removed from all the . . . muddle.'

'That's easy, then,' said Celyn, as Mam called us from the hallway and we clattered back downstairs. 'You need a friend and I need a friend. Simple as one and one makes two – put us together and we'll be sorted.'

And that's how we became inseparable – the same as Mam and Mistletoe. No big deal, no major discussion and decision, no fuss, no aggro – easy, obvious, comfortable and . . . yes, sorted. Quick as a flash and before I could blink. In the twinkling of two green, green eyes.

Gradually Mam relaxed her hold on me, lightened up and loosened the reins that had bound me too tight to her side ever since Dad left. She said being friends with Mistletoe took her out of herself, gave her a new lease of life. That was fine by me. She certainly didn't dwell on Dad and his failings and the terrible time we'd had so much – not every day, anyway, not so obsessively. It was a relief, I can tell you. I couldn't say we'd put it all behind us. I couldn't say we'd forgotten about it. I couldn't say everything was sugar and spice, perfectly nice and all that kind of rot. But . . . but there was a slight change. It was as if we'd been through a long, long night or the harshest of winters and, all at once, there were unexpected breaks in the darkness – a hint of dawn on the horizon, the occasional shaft of pale sunshine piercing the gloom. There were moments when we could just . . . relax, catch a glimpse of light at the end of the tunnel, if you know what I mean.

Each day, after Mam had done her chores and Sioned had been to playgroup, they both went over to the Midwinter house. Mam was helping Mistletoe make new puppets and repair old puppets ready for the summer shows. Sioned sat on the floor under the big table playing with scraps of fabric, skeins of silk, building towers of cotton reels, sorting through a biscuit tin full of all the buttons imaginable. She pottered, muttered make-believe games to herself, while Mam and Mistletoe stuffed and stitched, pasted and painted, nailed and nattered above her. Sometimes Celyn would play with Sioned, take her out into the little walled garden that sloped up the hill behind their house. I couldn't always be there, you see, but Celyn didn't have to go to school – lucky thing. She said she was 'an otherwise'. Both Mistletoe and Celyn seemed completely otherwise to me – so utterly unusual, so vibrantly strange – but what 'otherwise' meant was that Celyn could have her lessons at home.

'We're never in one place long enough for me to settle into an ordinary school,' said Celyn, 'and Mistletoe likes to teach me different things too . . . on top of the normal school lessons.'

Yeah, right, I thought. *Like circus skills and puppet making and . . . and . . .* I couldn't quite put my finger on exactly what Celyn seemed to learn from Mistletoe *. . . and a certain something extra-special, I suppose, a sort of merriment and life-changing magic.*

They both had that hard-to-pin-down quality, anyhow, and they both passed a part of it on to other people they met. I could tell that – even back then.

I'd have liked to visit as often as Mam and Sioned but, unlike Celyn, I had to go to school on weekdays. Still, it was becoming less of an ordeal. The other children were curious about the Midwinters. Their arrival had caused quite a stir in the town. They were a new interest, a constant topic of conversation and speculation. My family and its troubles were no longer at the forefront of their minds.

Mam said we'd been a nine days' wonder and everyone now had fresh fish to fry and about time too. Sometimes I told the others about the latest puppets Mam and Mistletoe had made. They were all looking forward to seeing the summer shows.

January, February, March and way into April – it felt like a preparation time, a waiting time, an odd in-between time. Change bubbled and brewed, uncoiled and grew beneath the surface. The harsh-beaked crows still perched on our front railings every morning, shadow-shaped our skies, churned our chimney every evening but the days were gradually lengthening, lightening. My blackest of black moods lifted, slowly shifted . . . little by little.

Now and again, the cries of crows were lost beneath the calls of sea birds. Drowned by Sioned's giggles, or Mam humming happily along to a CD, or Celyn shouting my name from the street the moment I'd got in from school – demanding I go out and play at once, that minute and no excuses. There just wasn't time to stay miserable when Mistletoe and Celyn were about. Sometimes I forgot to listen to that droning dirge of crows for hours altogether. Sometimes I even forgot to think about Dad – wiped him from my mind as if he'd never been part of us. We were lightening up . . . bit by bit, trying to move forward. Our life was gradually . . . improving.

Then Easter came and the past caught up with us. Slapped us in the face, punched us in the stomach, took us by the scruff of the neck and shook us all out of our fragile contentment. I'd so looked forward to those holidays from school, to spending each day with Celyn – but their end was abominable, worse than my worst imaginings, the most terrifying time of my life.

Things started so well. Celyn and I made the most of our time together. We flew kites on the beach, trekked across the sands at low tide to the next bay and picnicked while dabbling our feet in that ice-cold stream that runs down to the sea. We played pin-ball in the amusement arcade and visited the car-boot sale that had just restarted for the season. We went with Mam and Sioned to the local swimming pool, to the cinema, and with Mistletoe to a garden open day where she treated us to cream teas. Mistletoe and Celyn knew a lot about gardens – the names of trees and shrubs, flowers and herbs tripped off their tongues. They fingered leaf-buds gently, tipped the petal faces of primroses, of hidden violets, considered each strong shoot or subtle scent. Evergreens formed a backdrop, lined their path as they explored. Boughs waved, bent over them, wreathed closer until Mistletoe and Celyn, in their garments of grass and leaf and stem, merged . . . became invisible, lost in greenery. Sioned chased after them, tracked them in a game of hide-and-seek through a dappled maze of lime-green light and bottle-green shade.

Those days were luminous and the evenings yawned and stretched lazily as Celyn and I practised our skateboarding techniques after tea. Celyn became more skilful by the day.

'I love it,' she said. 'A sport where you can use your imagination. A sport where you can make up the moves. A sport where you're not kept hemmed in by white lines on the ground.'

Our skateboarding got faster, more daring. Sometimes we fell – but we learned to relax and tuck our elbows in and roll . . . and we learned to crouch low on the board so we didn't fall far. Soon we were both doing wheelies and kickturns – egging each other on – although Celyn was the first to manage an ollie. She just suddenly leapt – right there in front of me – dropped into a slope, then flew into the air for a moment with the board still pressed to her feet. I was so envious that we practised on and on that evening until I could do one too. Then I walked her home across the town to meet up with Mam and Sioned. Mistletoe gave us dandelion and burdock to drink while I waited for them to be ready. It slipped down a treat after all our hard work. The tall glasses were cold and misted like frost.

'How come you're streaking ahead at skateboarding when you've only just started?' I groaned. 'You can do everything, anything . . .'

'I'm used to balancing, you see,' Celyn said. 'After

all, I can walk on stilts, ride a unicycle, cross a tightrope, stand up straight on an acrobat's shoulders. When I was younger, we travelled for a while with a circus. Balancing is as natural as breathing to me. I don't even think about it. You wait – Mistletoe's going to buy me my own board next week. Then you'll have to look out!'

She skipped across the top of the high wall at the rear of her garden to demonstrate her excellent balancing skills, swinging the skateboard from one hand to the other as she went. She made me giddy. Once, I'd thought that life with Dad around was like trying to walk on a tightrope, a balancing act – but I'd imagined it as a tightening in the chest, a dry-mouthed and desperate attempt to remain upright, to be . . . to appear . . . kind of . . . normal. Celyn made life seem so straightforward, so easy, so different and such . . . fun.

My skills as a puppeteer didn't improve at all after my first attempt. I couldn't imitate the necessary voices to save my life. My puppet strings tangled themselves into knots and tripped up the whole show. And as for the juggling – try as I might, I simply couldn't juggle for toffee.

'Maybe you should be a clown,' suggested Mam once, watching me drop the umpteenth ball Celyn tossed me.

I took notice of all Celyn's handy hints. I tried keeping to only two balls. I tried shouting 'Throw!' as I released each of the balls and 'Catch!' when, now and then and only very occasionally, I managed to catch one of them. I tried to remember not to throw the second ball too low. But it was still no good. I couldn't juggle with balls, I couldn't juggle with clubs. I couldn't spin plates on a stick or master the twirl and flick of a diabolo. I attempted all of them. I honestly tried everything. I gritted my teeth and repeated that saying to myself:

If at first you don't succeed,
Try, try again.

And I tried and tried, again and again, but it was still no use and I still couldn't juggle.

Mam called me 'butter fingers' and fell about laughing.

'I think even Sioned might be better at throwing and catching things than me,' I admitted eventually. 'Perhaps it'd be best to stick with the skateboarding . . .'

And no one disagreed with me.

I stayed as far away as possible from the harbour, but I could see it from my bedroom window. There, Dad slouched in a canvas chair, half-heartedly touting tickets for his boat trips around the bay, for his mackerel-fishing excursions. Dad hadn't prepared properly for the new season. I could see that. Any idiot could see that. The paint on his boat was peeling. The hull was dangerously half-patched. Beer cans and take-away cartons littered the deck. His offers of outings obviously weren't tempting the spring tourists. They walked straight past him and his grimy advertising board. They ignored his on-its-last-legs boat and boarded one of the gleaming pleasure craft moored nearby – with their temptations of on-board toilets and iced drink machines and eager Jolly-Jack-

Tar captains who smiled instead of glowering at the customers and offered a helping hand to steady them on board from the quayside. There was nothing steady about Dad. Mam said he was a disgrace, a hopeless case. But she shrugged and said it quite cheerily – as if he was nothing to do with her any more. She said she'd washed her hands of him.

'Good riddance to bad rubbish,' Mam said.

It's not as simple as that, though, is it? I thought. *How can I be nothing to do with my dad? I can't rub out that connection, can I? It's not something that will ever go away – even if I want it to.*

Chapter 6

'Hedd! Get over here, boy. I want to talk to you!'

I nearly died.

It was the final evening of the school holiday. Celyn and I were skateboarding as usual along the front. The wind was picking up, so we'd just put our jackets on. Celyn kicked off first along the path in front of me on her new board. Her hair whipped in the breeze – it rayed out around her head red as sunset, startling as a halo. I'd been concentrating so hard on carving in a wide swoop past the telephone box and following Celyn's spiky-green, blown leaf spiral – spin – twist lead, with all the intricate series of wheelies and kickturns that were involved, that I'd failed to notice Dad coming up the hill.

He stood on the opposite side of the road, right outside our front door, swaying slightly and shouting his big mouth off. I felt my face flush as scarlet as Celyn's hair. I felt sick.

Please, Dad, I thought. *Not now, not right in front of Celyn.*

'Don't you dare ignore me! Not if you know what's good for you, you little . . .'

Dad's voice slurred, grew louder and more angry. A couple of elderly holiday-makers turned to stare at him. Mrs Price-Owen was at the glazed door of the newsagent's locking up for the night. I saw her purse her thin lips and shake her head in disgust before she pulled the blind down. Mrs Price-Owen and my dad had had words before about the paper bills. Mrs Price-Owen always called my mam 'that poor dab'.

'Hedd! Hedd . . . son!'

His voice made my skin crawl – raucous as a crow, some puppet's crazed swozzle-cry and dreadful as a death knell. He lurched, leaned back against the railings. A gang of other kids were laughing and joking in the distance, heading up from the square. I was shaking. I studied the ground, didn't know what to do for the best. The first volley of raindrops prickled the back of my neck. I shivered and . . . slowly . . . dragged . . . my feet towards him. He had that sort of effect, you see. Always got his own way.

Celyn caught my arm.

'Go home,' I muttered under my breath. 'Just get away from here.'

'Not likely,' said Celyn. She slipped her hand into mine and squeezed hard. I glanced at her. She appeared so confident, so determined and fearless. Her chin jutted defiantly. Her green eyes were cold.

'Come on,' she said, 'you can ignore him. We'll just walk right past.'

We crossed the road. I kept my back to Dad, tried to blot out his howled threats. All at once, Dad lunged forward, loomed over us. He grabbed at the hood of my jacket – and missed. As he stumbled, Celyn yanked my hand and we fled. We clattered through my front gate and took the steps two at a time. Mam must have heard the commotion because she was there at the door. We tumbled into the house and Mam tried to slam the door shut again behind us. Dad's rage was hot on our heels. His beery breath and curses surrounded us. He thumped the door inwards against the wall. Mam jumped back and screeched at him like a mad woman. Glass smashed, showered over us. The narrow hall was filled with bodies: me and Celyn, Mam and Dad, and Sioned. It was a war zone, a battleground and Sioned was in the middle of it. Little Sioned, stuck in the thick of things, being trampled underfoot. And Dad didn't care and Mam didn't notice. There was Sioned – only knee high to a grasshopper, after all – crying and crying as I'd never known her cry before. Crying fit to burst, crying as if her heart would break. Mam and Dad continued to hurl insults. Dad said we were his kids. Dad said he had rights. Mam said he wasn't fit to see us. Mam said he could whistle for his rights. Celyn stood on the stairs and yelled at them to stop but both of them ignored her.

I stared at Celyn's indignant fury. I stared at Mam's misery and Dad's desperation. I stared down at my small sister. Sioned was crying and pleading – just as I used to do. Then I saw it coming. I saw Dad raise his fist again. Mam flinched away and Sioned squirmed herself between them. She was crying and pleading – just as I used to do.

There was a flash of lightning and the whole scene was washed in an eerie green light. Then the hall spun red:

77

Suddenly Dad was in the street. I can't quite remember exactly how I got him out but it was brutal and bloody and you wouldn't want to go there. Enough was enough. I'd known I had to stop it – once and for all.

'And don't come back,' I screamed after him as he slunk across the street. He slumped on the bench. He was beaten and bedraggled – unrecognisable. He certainly wasn't my jolly old dad any more. He wasn't even my bad-tempered, brawling dad any more. He was a broken thing. He was weeping, calling out he was sorry.

'Nothing new there then,' I shouted. 'You're always sorry . . . afterwards. You're always sorry when it's too late. Sorry's only a word to you . . . and you have to give us more than words. Words alone can be . . . too easy, too . . . cheap.'

Rain poured down his face, soaked his black T-shirt. He looked . . . dumped, like an abandoned rubbish sack. He hunched there, ghastly as a goblin, a pathetic Mr Punch, a mockery of a man.

'Hedd! Hedd, don't say those things. Hedd . . . son . . . you're killing me.'

'Great!' My mouth filled with rainwater. I gasped and sputtered, gulped it all down. 'Great! Do us all a favour, Dad. Just crawl away and die!'

I turned my back on him. I kicked shut the shattered door. I ran past Mam, past Sioned, past Celyn, up to my room.

I sprawled on my bed. For a long time I couldn't stop shaking and shivering although I wasn't cold.

When Mam came to see if I was OK, I wouldn't speak to her. I couldn't be bothered with it all any more. I was worn out, exhausted, at the end of my tether – in a state of shock, I suppose. Mam brought a tray up – told me to eat. She said it'd make me feel better. Yeah, right. What is it with mothers and food? I curled in a tight ball, faced the wall and refused to answer her. Eventually, she left the tray on the floor beside my bed, stroked my hair as if I were a baby and went away. I wouldn't, couldn't talk. Some things are unspeakable, aren't they? At least, they seem that way when they're fresh – when they're taking over, flooding your mind. I didn't want to see anyone or be with anyone – not Sioned, not even Celyn. I couldn't get rid of Dad, though. He was still with me. I remembered the look on his face when I'd wished him dead. It kept coming back to me – over and over again – and my words haunted me. *Would I have stood up to Dad in that way if Celyn hadn't been there or if she hadn't caught my eye? Or had it been to do with Sioned?*

I didn't know, and thinking about it simply made me tired, more tired than I'd ever been in my life.

Crows cawed outside the window, cawed and cawed, their cries growing louder and louder until it was as if they were right inside the room with me, as if I'd summoned them. More and more crows crowded in, a murder, a great buffeting cloud of birds. The beat of their wings was a wild wind rising. They fluttered their feathers like shadow puppets, made a flickering ebb and flow of storm waves that lapped over my floor, bed, walls – breakered against my ceiling. The crows cawed on and on, drowned me in night. They frightened me – yet my outburst against Dad seemed to have invited them closer. I pulled the duvet over my head. I felt as if I was being sucked under a vast sea, was plunging right to the bottom of the deepest, dark ocean. I couldn't be bothered to struggle any longer. I sank down – way, way down – into unimaginable gloom, a blankness blacker than black. I was silent – words, cries welled up but were trapped in my throat. I could hardly breathe. Tears ran into my mouth. I gulped their salt, drank their sorrow – until, at last, I slept.

My mind wouldn't rest. It filled with dreams, nightmares – jostled images turning in a whirlpool, muddled snippets of action, phrases that repeated over and over in my brain. At the start, I looked like a holiday poster – all happy in shorts and sunglasses, surfing the sea against a sky of postcard blue. I so wanted to be that boy. I so wanted to be . . . ordinary. But everything altered. A storm overtook me, caught me up like a twister and I was trapped in a nightmare.

Crows, wind, storm blasted into my world. Water streamed against my face. The wind flayed my body, howled past my ears. I skidded across icy waves on my skateboard, dropped in on the impossible curves of mountainous seas. One minute my heart was in my mouth – the next it sank to my boots. I was struggling to keep my balance, trying to hold it together. It was a roller-coaster, a helter-skelter ride on the switch-backed tide. My head, arms and legs jerked and jigged faster and faster in clumsy desperation. My movements grew more extreme, more erratic – way beyond my control. My head spun like a top, my arms flailed like twin windmills and my poor legs turned to jelly. It was as if I was a puppet – not a real person at all. I pranced in a grotesque and dangerous dance on the end of my strings. I was tugged down deep as a submarine, towed across rips, flung high from a wave ramp in an aerial loop. I screamed. Crows screeched in reply. Their dark-hand wings were outstretched towards me.

Dad was always with me and I was always with Dad. Dad and me, me and Dad – all stirred up yet always together. One moment I was drowning – the next it was Dad. I clung to him like a lifesaver, hung on him like a lead weight and vice versa, round and round about. Down we'd plummet to Davy Jones's locker. Down we'd go to feed the fishes. Then up we'd bubble like air, buoyant as corks on the swell. Sometimes Dad would stay stuck, anchored in the depths. Sometimes he'd swim, swift as a seal, to the surface. I was helpless, at the mercy of the elements, the rampage of rain, wind and water. Lightning flicked different pictures – jumpy as an old newsreel. Everything was topsy-turvy, at odds with itself, as tangled up as . . . spaghetti.

Then the crows whirled closer, swirled and skirled, encircled my head like a crown. The images changed once more. I grew tall. I was godlike. I could work wonders and wizardry. My power was awesome and I was in charge of the whole show. I could truly do anything. I could conjure a thunderclap, create a flash of lightning, crash the sea wall to rubble and wash away a lighthouse. Life and death were my playthings. I could cause a shipwreck or bring a boat safely home to harbour. All hope was in my hands, foul-play and failure my fault. At long last, I pulled the strings.

'Roll up, roll up, roll up,' I shouted.

'Caw, caw, caw,' croaked my coronet of crows.

I threw my head back and roared with laughter. The flimsy backdrop of bay and town trembled. I was the Professor, the great puppet-master.

A clap of thunder, directly overhead, jerked me awake. I sat up in bed – aching, still disorientated. Midnight by my Man-U clock. A real storm raged. A humdinger. A right 'pepper pot' buster.

Shouts in the street outside. Racing footsteps. I lifted the edge of the blind. Saw: a thrash of crow's-nest trees, blown sheets of rain, jet night spot-lit by street lamps. Shadow men, shadow women – a confused puppetry of people. Their black shapes flickered, were splashed by flashlight. Sudden lightning showed white spray high above the harbour wall, an inky churn of ocean.

The flare's burst made me jump. I watched it blaze, fade over the life-boat station. Even as I watched, the life-boat surged into the sea, slapped the crests of the first waves. When I was a little kid, Dad and I sometimes watched the life-boat go out. He held me tight on his shoulders – so I could see properly. It was exciting then – not at all scary. I swallowed. Everywhere so wet – and my mouth was so dry.

Then there was a hammering at our ruined front door. The plump-thump of Mam's slippered feet quick on the stairs. A babble of voices in our hallway – and my dad's name rising to the surface again and again. My dad's name bubbling from everyone's lips. My dad's name tossed around like flotsam on the rise and fall of words.

Dad, I thought to myself. *Dad, you stupid fool. Don't tell me you've taken that death-trap of a boat, that hopeless old rust-bucket, out to sea. Not on a night like this . . . and you in such a state. I didn't mean it. Please . . . please, don't go and die on me.*

I leant my head against the cold windowpane. Ghost crows tumbled through the glass into my room. They blew right in like cinders. They were tiny, bat-like, their caws sharp but muted. Their spread wing-tips were like fingers and scratched at my chilled face.

'Murderer!' They croaked their cracked cry as they wheeled closer, ever closer. 'You . . . murderer!'

I swung my window open and the crows swooped out into the night. The sound of their wings in my ears was like panic rising . . . my heart's fierce beating, my blood pounding.

For a moment, I thought I saw Mistletoe standing tall and still and straight as a wand on the bench opposite our house. She was raised higher than the busy crowd that had gathered and milled about her. She towered over them. She looked . . . as sturdy and as strong as a lighthouse ought to be. Only her head moved as she scanned the pitch-dark and pitching seas. Motes of light – emerald, silver, gold – shimmered around her, spread out to spangle the gloom. From across the bay, way out in the far, far, north, a twinkling of stars – first yellow, then white, then bright, bright green – seemed to answer her. I blinked, rubbed my eyes, and she was gone.

Next day, we went to visit Dad in hospital. He seemed smaller, shrunken somehow, propped up in bed on pillows in the corner of the ward. His skin was sort of shrivelled – like how your fingertips go when you've stayed in the bath water for too long. He was as wrinkly as one of those droopy-faced dogs or an ancient great-great-grandad, or a prune. He was quieter than usual too, at first. It was as if he was somewhere far away – and almost not my dad at all.

'Well, you certainly gave us quite a fright,' said Mam, dumping a polythene bag of grapes we'd brought on the bedside cabinet. Sioned stared at Dad as if he were a stranger, her eyes wide and as dark as the grapes she slowly picked and popped, one-by-one, into her mouth.

'My boat . . .' Dad's voice shook. His hands fluttered, fragile as feathers against the sharp, white sheet.

'Blow the boat,' Mam said. 'I always said that boat was bad news and it swallowed money like a drain. The seabed's welcome to the old tub. It was as full of holes as a colander, a sieve. Fast as you patched one leak, it sprang another one. You could've died . . .'

'D'you think anyone would've cared . . . or noticed, come to that?'

'Oh, for goodness sake! Just listen to yourself. Of course . . . people . . . would care. You've got Sioned and Hedd worrying about you, for a start, and even I was . . . frantic. We had half the neighbourhood in our house concerned for you last night. Total drama.'

'Mmm.' Dad didn't sound convinced but then, after a long moment, he squinted sideways at Sioned and me.

'Sorry,' he said.

And strangely enough, against all the odds, it was a start. I'd long ago given up on Dad's apologies. He was always saying sorry but he never acted sorry, never, ever changed – but . . . this apology . . . this one was different. This one was a turning point. This time he actually – and for the first time ever in his entire life – meant it.

'I'm so, so sorry . . . truly,' Dad mumbled again. He looked sheepish – kind of guilty and squashed. Then, all at once, a floodtide of words: 'I've been to Hell and back and I know I dragged you all along with me for the ride. I hit rock-bottom and I'm so ashamed, I can't tell you. But now I've been given another chance . . . and you're all here supporting me and I don't deserve that . . . and I know . . . I know this means I've got to change. Get a grip, clean up my act and so on . . . and I will – honestly. At least, I will try . . . try my hardest, give it my best shot.'

It was a bit squirmy, what with the tears in his eyes

and the way he put his arm around me and so on. I listened to him rambling on and part of me thought:

Yeah, yeah. Pull the other one, it's got bells on.

But he had nearly drowned, after all, and lost his precious boat and everything – so I kept my mouth shut and put a polite mask on my face as if I believed him. Sioned didn't appear to be listening and just sucked another grape silently into her mouth. Only Mam smiled encouragingly. She had the same strained look about her that mothers have at their children's sports day or when they're performing at an eisteddfod and aren't very good – you know, sort of anxious and agonised but trying to be supportive.

People say that 'seeing is believing' and 'the proof of the pudding is in the eating' and 'actions speak louder than words'. That's what I was waiting for – for Dad to pull himself together and make a real difference to our lives. It felt as if I'd been waiting for that forever. I didn't want his make-believe, his fairy tales or his lies. I was fed up to the back teeth with excuses and sob-stories. I was tired of praying for a turn-around. I'd had it up to here with living my life holding my breath.

I felt so tense, so uptight, so furious . . . and then:

What have I got to lose? I suddenly thought. *I might as well give him one . . . absolutely final . . . chance. Just so long as he leaves Sioned out of it. Last night I thought I was a murderer – and that was the worst feeling in the world, the pits. So why not play along with him, Hedd? Go for it . . . one last throw of the dice, one last spin of the wheel. If he doesn't make it this time, it'll be over between Dad and me . . . curtains.*

I picked up one of the few remaining grapes in the bag and popped it into Dad's mouth instead of my own. He was so startled that he swallowed it whole and it made him sputter and cough.

Mam tut-tutted: 'Finish him off, why don't you?'

But Dad's eyes met mine and we knew we'd made a pact – a hand-on-heart, cut-my-throat-and-hope-to-die promise to each other. A solemn vow of humungous effort and patience and . . . well . . . love and trust and a whole bucket load of cheesy carry-ons, I suppose. The shift between us came like a bolt from the blue and was almost against my better judgement.

Dad did seem different, though, strangely sea-changed. Since I'd stood up to him, we were more . . . equal. The only thing that was left for us to do was stick with it. I knew I'd hang in there. I knew I'd try anything. But Dad? I blinked swiftly. My eyes were hurting and I had to rub them with my knuckles. Dad's face on the pillow was misted in a haze of silvery gold light, the iron bedstead flared with green-tinged brightness. My eyes were wet. I wiped them quickly on my sleeve in case anyone noticed. Dad swam back into focus.

I told myself there was nothing else to be done . . . I could only wait and see.

Chapter 7

The next few months were easier. Dad was released from hospital quite quickly and the loss of his boat – sad as it was – seemed to help him to take stock, forced him into making changes in his life. The relationship between Dad and myself had altered since our set-to on the night of the storm. We were careful with each other, wary. Often I felt we behaved in a similar way to strange dogs when they meet for the first time – you know, walking around each other all stiff-legged and cautious while keeping their eyes firmly fixed on each other's behaviour.

But careful's got to be better than careless, hasn't it? I told myself.

A new routine started. Most Sundays, Dad would take Sioned and me for fish and chips at the beach café. He'd let us chose a cornet each afterwards and we'd eat them walking along the harbour wall together. I always had mint-choc-chip and Sioned always had blackcurrant – which was a mistake, if you ask me, because blackcurrant's a deep, stainy colour and Sioned can manage to make more of a mess with blackcurrant than any other choice of flavour. Dad didn't seem fazed. He'd hold Sioned's sticky-drippy hand and read the old custom dues list to her from the harbour wall. He'd lift her up in his arms to see the dolphins if they happened to be performing in the bay. He'd often put one arm on my shoulder, too, as we stood together – silently looking out towards Enlli from the exact spot where the old pepper-pot-shaped lighthouse had made its last stand. I tried to relax under the weight of his arm. It was hard. I had to concentrate and blank images from the past. I had to force myself . . . to try . . . to wipe the slate clean and start over. Often Celyn would join us later in the afternoon. We'd demonstrate our skateboarding skills to Dad, show off our latest stunts. Dad had managed to get taken on for some shifts at the whelk-packing, so he smelt rather whiffy if we ever met up with him before he'd been home to change. None of us were really worried about that, although we teased him sometimes. He'd done worse things in the old days than stink of whelks, after all.

Count your blessings, Hedd, I told myself, trying not to sniff if I was standing close by him.

Mam offered to put his work clothes through our washing machine because he didn't have one up at the caravan. Dad accepted and said it was kind of her. Mam and Dad were like that after the night of the storm – very calm and collected and reasonable with each other. I knew Mam had heard all his good intentions before and I could guess she was still thinking:

Tell me the old, old story . . .
and
Promises, promises . . .
and
A leopard never changes its spots . . .

But his nearly drowning had shaken her, so she buttoned her lip and kept any thoughts of that sort to herself. She made no comment about chips or ice cream either – and that was a first. Sioned and I just had to eat our way through extra vegetables on Saturday and a banquet-sized feast of salad and fruit every Monday to make up for Dad's idea of Sunday lunch.

Dad continued assuring us he'd turned over a new leaf. He kept apologizing – especially to me – again and again and again. He vowed that . . . if we gave him a chance and some space and a little time then . . . everything would work out fine.

Always jam tomorrow, never jam today, I'd thought nastily – but I didn't say anything. I kept my polite mask in place. I wasn't going to pass judgement at that stage. I was biding my time and waiting to see how things panned out.

Still, fair play, I thought. *He is at least making more effort this time. It's been a while since he's lost it.*

Another saying kept reeling through my mind though: *There's many a slip 'twixt cup and lip.*

I just couldn't quite relax. I just couldn't quite believe in him or completely trust him again. And who could blame me? We'd all been so damaged.

Although he was getting used to Celyn, Dad still found Mistletoe awkward to deal with. I suppose she was way out of his experience . . . but then, Mistletoe's way out of most people's experience. Mam said Mistletoe was a one-off, Mistletoe was an original, unique.

Mam said: 'They threw away the mould when they made Mistletoe.'

Dad said: 'I thought you were supposed to be like twins. I thought the two of you were soul-mates.'

At that time, Dad still seemed to have to struggle not to be jealous of the new closeness between Mam and Mistletoe. Mistletoe was certainly something else. Once, I'd thought that Celyn might grow up to be like her. They were similar in so many ways, but Celyn was dreamier and quieter than Mistletoe. She was still vibrant and special but . . . rather different too, completely . . . herself. Ending up like your parents is a worrying idea, isn't it? People say Sioned takes after Mam. They do look vaguely alike but the comparison's usually made when they're both chattering away as if there's no tomorrow. Back then, it really concerned me. Back then, I hoped against hope that I wouldn't end up being exactly the same as my dad. You wouldn't wish that on your worst enemy, would you? I decided I really only wanted to grow up to be myself – you know, as singular as Mistletoe . . . but not single as in completely alone. Ever since Celyn had come to town, I'd discovered that it wasn't such a bad thing after all to have a friend – especially if life was getting you down. There was something in that saying 'a trouble shared is a trouble halved' after all, I'd found. Well, it wasn't quite as much baloney as I'd thought, anyhow.

One day, about a month after he'd come out of hospital, Mistletoe rang Dad on his mobile and asked him to do her a small favour. I happened to be with him up at the caravan at the time and he was tightening the trucks on my board for me. I could tell that he was reluctant to help Mistletoe but, in his new role as a reformed character, was trying his best to seem pleasant. I had the suspicion that he was probably struggling to appear extra-well-behaved in front of me. Mistletoe asked Dad if he'd mind picking up some more honey supplies – for herself and Celyn and also for Mam and me and – most of all – Sioned.

'. . . And apart from being divinely delicious . . . honey's such a magical, healing product, isn't it?'

Even I could hear Mistletoe's enthusiastic trilling – and I was sitting at the other end of the caravan to the phone. I listened to Dad sighing a lot, yet obviously feeling obliged to agree – once he could get a word in edgeways. I smiled to myself. One nil to Mistletoe.

As it turned out, that trip to the Honey Farm was great news for Dad, as he landed another part-time job. It wasn't just the added income that made a difference, either. Dad loved the work there. Sometimes he had to help in the souvenir shop, sometimes in the cafe. Sometimes he had to explain the displays to visitors or get involved with maintenance work – grass cutting, weeding, painting and so on. He liked chatting to the tourists again. He enjoyed sharing his knowledge of, and his stories about, the surrounding area. The work that Dad loved best of all, however, was something quite new to him, something completely different. The most enjoyable thing of all for Dad was working with the bees. Dad took to being a beekeeper as a duck takes to water.

As the dandelions opened their sun faces and the apple trees blossomed, Dad became bedazzled by bees. Suddenly, Dad seemed to talk of nothing but bees. The lingering silence between us disappeared as Dad became honey-tongued. He always had something new to tell me each time we met. How he was helping to remove the frames from the beehives to check on each colony's condition. How he was clearing debris from the bottom boards ready for the new season. How he was keeping an eye peeled for early swarming.

Dad read library books about bees, he watched a DVD about bees, he logged onto web sites about bees, he put posters about bees all around the caravan and began to go to beekeepers' meetings. Dad talked so much about bees that Mam, Sioned and I felt as if we had bees buzzing out of our ears. Bees were my dad's salvation. The buzz he got from bees gave him the new direction he needed. Bees kept him busy. Now and then, Mam would laugh at him and say: 'Pleazzzz no more beezzzz!'

'Buzzy busy, busy buzzy bees!'

Sioned made up tongue-twisting songs. Mistletoe and Celyn helped her stitch a fat, felt bee puppet that bounced and bumbled along from an elastic string. Even I found myself bemused, found myself humming across the town to the Midwinter house with a hop-skip-jump of my bee-striped trainers.

Bee keeping was the bee's knees as far as Dad was concerned. He wrote a list for me in my notebook of the types of plants bees like to visit when they're gathering nectar:

crocus and pussy willow
maple blossom and raspberry
tulip, locust, orange
alfalfa and clover
sunflower, fireweed
buckwheat or thistle
basswood, aster, loosestrife.

The plant names flowed sweetly when I read the list aloud: a sunny verse, a waggle-dance of words.

The months flew by on bees' wings. In June, Dad was adding supers to the hives and keeping both eyes peeled for swarming and explaining about queen bees and royal jelly.

Sioned drew a picture of a bee in a crown and Mam had to keep making us strawberry jelly for tea – which might be Sioned's favourite but, honestly, isn't the same thing as royal jelly at all.

In July, Dad told us he was checking the honey flow was developing properly and watching out for whitewax along the edges of the top bars – which would mean a hive was overcrowded. Sometimes Celyn and I would go to the Honey Farm with him. We sat a safe distance away on the bank and watched him work at the hives. He looked like a spaceman in his bee-suit and veil. He moved slowly, deliberately, at his tasks, puffed gentle clouds of smoke to pacify the bees. His hands made calm movements. They wafted across each hive as if casting a spell, as if giving a blessing. Watching him brought a picture of Mistletoe into my mind. I'd seen her hands work that magic. It was ages since my dad had stayed so quiet, so patient, so . . . measured . . . for so long. It was ages since he'd appeared so peaceful and . . . content.

Celyn and I were beginning to skate everything in the street and the longer evenings when I returned from school meant we had more time to perfect our moves. We could both pop ollies with no probs at all. Let me give you guys a tip – when you start to try tricks on a skateboard, you have to commit. That's what Celyn and I learned, anyway. There's no point being half-hearted or pussy-footing around. If you don't commit yourself to making that trick work – then you're sure to fall. If you get out there and go for it – you're much more likely to pull it off. Celyn and I were doing street style skating. We were basically making it up as we went along, but we'd found we could use an ollie to get up onto a low metal rail at one end of the park. Once there – and it took quite a few sessions to make it, I can tell you – we were able to do long, spectacular grinds, metal on metal. Never mind about bees – that was our top buzz. We'd grab the boards and twist ourselves back down onto the path. Soon we were practising the same stunt – over and over – on every suitable surface we could find.

Mistletoe and Mam were working flat out to complete all the new puppets and props they needed for the summer. Mistletoe and Mam, Celyn and myself and even Sioned were going to have special costumes too.

Mistletoe insisted we'd all be involved. Mistletoe said it was all hands to the pumps.

Mam was in her element – she was a different woman to the mam I'd always known – up to her elbows in silks and satins, up to her eyes in buttons and bows. Designing and cutting out, sewing and trimming.

'Marian!' called Mistletoe twenty times a day. 'Can you help me with this?'

Or that . . . or whatever.

'How did we ever cope without you, Marian?'

Mam basked in the praise. Mam became happier, more . . . confident . . . with each passing hour. She'd already made a new and amazing hat for Mistletoe to wear for the shows – all her own idea, all her own work. It was green, of course. It would hardly have suited Mistletoe otherwise, would it? It was a magical hat – an intricate patchwork of textures and tones. Its crown towered – magnificent as a mountain. Its brim spread wide – broad as lush meadowlands. It was beaded, beribboned, encrusted . . . exquisite. There was a hint of sea-shimmer about it – a crystalline stream-sparkle, a blaze of sun and star shine, a sheen of moonlight. Feathers curled tall and bowery as summer woodland, were spiked with conifers of hat-pins. There were bunches of scarlet and pearl berries. Crimson and cream petals twined in delicate sprays. It was all seasons. It was evergreen. It was a landscape of a hat.

Mam and Mistletoe said they intended to perform at all the local agricultural shows as well as every fine day on the beach. Celyn told me she and Mistletoe usually travelled about more extensively. They usually covered large festivals as well as performing on much busier tourist beaches. Apparently, Mistletoe had decided to take a year out, had planned a quieter interlude in one place, in our town.

'For a change,' she'd told Celyn.

'She said we were needed here,' said Celyn, 'and I can see that.'

She sucked thoughtfully on a strand of hair. 'Mistletoe said she could do with recharging her own batteries too. I suppose I do often catch her standing peacefully late at night – gazing way out to sea.'

'I've seen her too from my bedroom window,' I said. 'She stands there like a lighthouse or . . . or a beacon . . . as if she's part of a relay of light.'

Celyn considered for a moment. 'Mmm . . . it seems to fill her with a weird power. Sometimes she almost sparkles and crackles with . . . with energy.'

Celyn studied the town, the harbour, the cauldron of the bay rimmed by mountains, jewelled by Enlli.

'I've quite enjoyed staying in one place for a while, myself. It's been a new experience for me. I'm not saying I'd want to do it all the time – I'd probably get to feel a right stick in the mud and become restless. Still,' – she glanced up at me, her face elfin, mischievous beneath her berry-bright fringe – 'it's pretty nice to be stuck in the mud with a hippopotamus of a friend for a while. It's OK having a good friend, isn't it?'

'Hmmm . . . '

'Hey!' Celyn dug me in the ribs.

'What? Yeah . . . I mean, of course it's great to be

friends with you. I'd just . . . well, I'd just never really imagined you leaving again, that's all.'

'Don't worry about it! We're not going to vanish all at once into thin air. I'm sure Mistletoe will give us fair warning when the time's right. But . . . Mistletoe does say all things have their season . . .'

I jumped up from the bench and kicked off on my board down the hill. Celyn raced after me, carving the path, popping ollies on each straight run. I waved to Josh, Aled and Owain as they carried their own boards towards the square. Aled had his younger brother in tow. He pulled a face, then grinned at me as I passed. I knew what he meant. Little kids! You love them and all that – but sometimes you'd rather be without. Especially when you're with your mates. Aled's mam was always getting him to mind his brother. Celyn and I sped on . . . left the boys far behind. We were laughing . . . but I felt odd, slightly sick. I'd never, ever thought about the Midwinters leaving again. Stupid, I know, but I was used to them being there – just across the bay.

How will I, how will Mam, how will Sioned manage without them if they go? I wondered.

I couldn't imagine it. I didn't think I could bear it. I realized then how much better our lives had become since that miserable night when I'd first seen them. They'd appeared out of the darkness when the world seemed desolate. I didn't want to return to that emptiness, that bleakness, that . . . despair. The mere thought of it terrified me.

Chapter 8

The summer shows were a blast. For once, the school holidays brought a long spell of warm, cloudless weather so, day after day, *The Midwinters' Grand Midsummer Extravaganza* performed on the beach. The town was heaving, the caravan park full – and tourists flocked to the sands. It couldn't have been better. It was the best time ever. It was . . . perfection.

Mistletoe was the puppet-mistress-of-ceremonies and she was gorgeously swathed in all-the-greens-of-summer silks. Mam and Celyn were her puppeteer assistants. Mam only had a small role in the performance but she was also the one who took care of our costumes, mended any damage to the cloth of the theatre or to the clothes the puppet characters wore. Mam helped with the setting up and the scenery. She made our daily picnic lunch. Mam said she was a backstage person at heart. She wore her ordinary shorts, sandals and T-shirt. At first I was disappointed she hadn't dressed up – but then I saw the sun hat she'd made herself. It was as pretty and perky as a parasol – and almost as big. It was a strutting-your-stuff-like-a-peacock sort of hat and it did Mam proud.

Celyn was not a backstage person at all – even though she wasn't quite as in-your-face as Mistletoe. Celyn was out there showing off her juggling tricks at the beginning and end of each show. Her role was to tempt the audience along, to send them home extra-happy.

Celyn wore a jester's cap Mam had made her with holly leaves that sprouted from its three pointed pinnacles and shiny, scarlet bells that jingled merrily as she moved. She had a loose jerkin in a red and green diamond pattern and a pair of short, emerald trousers that Mam had appliqued with more sprigs of holly. Her arms, lower legs and feet were bare – that was to keep her limbs free for juggling and also to help her stay cool. I thought Celyn was the coolest girl I'd ever seen. Her hair blazed even brighter than berries, flamed a hotter red than rubies, glowed and glistened like . . . well . . . 'like strawberry jelly full of sunshine' exactly as Sioned said.

When she'd been trying to encourage me to learn, Celyn had told me that long ago, in the Middle Ages, juggling was thought so special, so clever, that it was connected in people's minds with magic. The ability to juggle was seen as a sign of unearthly power.

When Celyn gave her juggling performances, I always recalled that. Her skills were marvellous, her speed miraculous, the whole effect . . . magical. She used soft, leather, bean-filled bags for juggling on the beach.

'They're safer than clubs if someone runs in the way,' she said.

The smaller kids, such as Sioned or Aled's brother, were always dodging about – and Mistletoe and Celyn didn't want them to be clunked with a club. The bean-filled bags didn't roll away either if one was dropped.

'And, of course,' Celyn added, 'there's no need at all for them to bounce when you're juggling on sand. It wouldn't work properly.'

Celyn's bean-bags were glossy – some red, some silver. Celyn started juggling with three of them – in a simple series of throw and catch actions. Simple as far as Celyn was concerned, that is. I still found the most basic throws impossible. Then she'd start to wind up the pace of the exchanges. Then she'd pick up more bean-bags until five, seven, even nine cascaded about her. She'd reverse the pattern of the cascade. She'd juggle with her eyes closed. That was always a good move and made the crowd cheer. Next she'd juggle single-handed. Then she'd pick up an even number of bean-bags and juggle a fountain pattern with no cross-over throws. Sometimes she'd juggle with an on-sync rhythm – with both hands throwing at the same time, sometimes with an off-sync rhythm – where each hand throws in turn. The red and silver colours spun and spun – faster than the eye could follow. Their individual shapes were lost. A mirage appeared – a silver ball of mistletoe, a red wreath of holly. By that stage, the audience would be going wild, cheering and clapping along. Sioned and I would be cheering and clapping too. Celyn finished her act with a succession of three bean-bag tricks. I'd shout out the names for those watching:

chops, fakes
milking the cow
three ball starts

above the head
Statue of Liberty
penguin, head rolls
pirouettes, multiplex.

Finally, Celyn would catch the bags – spin a few last body throws – and catch the bags again. She'd whip off her jingling juggling cap and her freed hair would spike out like a crimson dandelion seed-head as she took her bow.

Sioned would be beyond by that stage.

'Wow-eeee!' she'd shout. 'Wow-eeee!'

She'd race round and round the puppet theatre before joining me to collect the money in a golden top hat. Sioned's behaviour always made the crowd laugh – and both she and I were dressed as clowns, so it appeared to be part of our act. Sioned was all in pink with pom-poms. She was tickled pink too with her outfit – because pink was her favourite colour . . . and still is unfortunately. My own get-up was ludicrous. I had baggy trousers about a metre too large for my waist, and braces – I kid you not – braces holding them up. My wig had a bald patch in the centre and orange ringlets over each ear. I'd also been provided with a false red nose and spangly eye make-up . . . yes, you heard me correctly . . . eye make-up, together with a mad, lip-sticked grin. I had a pair of those long, long, long far-too-big shoes that clowns wear as well . . . oh, and a bow tie. The bow tie was OK. I could make it turn like a propeller and it had a secret squeezy bit, so I could squirt water at people. I supposed my costume was Mam's idea of a joke . . . you know, because I couldn't juggle.

Yeah, yeah . . . chuckle, chuckle . . . nice one, Mam, I thought.

My heart sank the first time I saw Josh, Owain and Aled walking across the beach to watch the show. I'd worried that they might laugh at me. You would imagine it, wouldn't you? What with my crazy costume and me playing Muppets with a bunch of females. They were all right, though – laughing with me, really, rather than at me. It makes a difference, doesn't it? They applauded the puppets, gasped at Celyn's juggling skills and even took it in good part when I dared to squirt them with my bow tie. Aled had his brother, Steffan, tagging along. Steffan roared round and round with Sioned, copying her shouts of 'Wow-eeee!' until they both fell over in a heap on the sand.

Those days on the beach weren't just fun because of the shows we did. The performances only took up part of the day. Celyn and I had time to change and swim in the sea or hold Sioned's hands and jump her again and again over the incoming waves. When there was a strong enough breeze, we'd launch our kites and make them carve and slide across the sky in skateboard-style stunts. We built rampart after rampart of towers in the sand for Sioned with her new bucket and spade, helped her dig moats and fill them with water. Celyn and I took turns with the spade and buried Aled up to his neck in the sand . . . and then dug him out again. We ate ice creams, had picnics, stayed late for evening barbecues. Sometimes, Aled, Owain, Josh, Celyn and I played games of football and cricket . . . while Steffan and Sioned got under our feet or ran away with the ball.

Once . . . only once . . . Celyn and I went on a boat trip, but that made me feel sad. It was lovely, in a way, don't get me wrong. The sea sparkled and dolphins leapt into their dance as if to order, as if purely for our pleasure. But being on that boat reminded me of Dad's old pride and joy wrecked at the bottom of the bay. It reminded me of all my past times with Dad – the good and the bad.

Dad himself didn't appear to be brooding too much. What with the whelks, the tourists and the bees – he hardly had a spare moment to brood any more. Late August was exciting for Dad. It was the first time he'd taken the honey crop. He was brim full of it – told us how he had to remove each loaded super from the hive, extract all the honey in a special extracting machine and then return the supers to the bee colony. We still saw quite a lot of him. He still found time . . . made time . . . to be involved in our everyday lives. He always helped take equipment for our performances to a show ground or took a turn at burning the barbecue sausages. Often, he'd join in our ball games or give Sioned and Steffan rides on his back – right into the waves. Once, he stayed and watched our performance all the way through. He cheered and clapped along with the rest of the audience. Afterwards, he put one arm around Sioned and one arm around me.

'Whatever have I done to deserve two such children?' he said. 'A son as bald as a turnip with seven-league sized feet . . . and a daughter as pink and as squealy as . . . as a piggy-wig!'

He cuddled us tight in case we'd not realized he was teasing us. I forgot to even think about pulling away. I forgot to hold myself tense and separate. I leaned close into his arm.

'Great hat, babe,' he said to Mam.

He gave her a saucy sort of wink as he watched her walk by. Mam smiled that shy smile that people use when they're embarrassed but pleased at the same time. It surprised me . . . caught me off guard.

Lately, Mam and Dad seem to be getting along, I thought. *In fact . . . lately . . . Mam and Dad seem to be getting along . . . rather well.*

I started watching them again, whenever they were together. I'd try to work them out. It began to get to me. One night, I mentioned it to Mam as we walked home. I simply had to . . . I couldn't hold everything inside any longer.

'Mam . . .'

'Ummm? . . .'

'Mam . . . d'you think . . . d'you think . . .'

It was surprisingly difficult to bring the subject up – even though the thoughts were filling my brain fit to burst and the words were scrabbling frantically on the tip of my tongue.

'What?' Mam was fumbling in the depths of her bag for her keys. Sioned was sitting on the top step, waiting. 'Do I think what? Has the cat got your tongue, Hedd? Spit it out!'

So I did.

'Do you think you and Dad will . . . you know . . . ever get back together again?'

I'd said it all in a rush and then I was left . . . empty . . . and holding my breath. At times I hold my breath when something fearful is about to happen. At times I hold my breath when something exciting is about to occur. I wasn't really sure which answer I hoped Mam would give. It was such a difficult, complicated one to call.

Mam laughed out loud.

'Oh Hedd! You are joking, aren't you? I know you're dressed up as a clown but . . . honestly! You of all people know . . . know what we've been through . . .'

I must have appeared startled, or disappointed, or extremely relieved. I couldn't tell you what my head was thinking – let alone what my face was showing.

Mam took one look at me and her voice became very soothing and quiet. She put her hands on my shoulders and turned me around gently. She crouched down so we were on the same level, head to head, face to face. Like you do with a little kid when they're hurt and you're being kind.

'It's never going to happen, Hedd. We're only just beginning to manage to behave well to each other now we're apart. I know we had other troubles . . . not much money coming in and so on . . . But . . . your dad . . . your dad and I . . . Well, let's simply say that neither of us is at our best when we're together all the time. It's not right. It doesn't work. It's not fair on anybody.'

I let out the breath.

So that's that, then, I thought. *No beating about the bush. No ifs, buts or maybes. It's all been spelt out to me. Now it's crystal clear and I know where I stand.*

I still wasn't sure how I felt. Not really and truly.

But it's good to know, isn't it? I told myself. *At least I'll be able to give up on all that . . . watching. It's easier not to have to go on wondering, and worrying, and carefully churning the same old thing over and over, round and round in my mind . . . like . . . like trying to juggle with some great, fragile glass bauble that I'm constantly terrified I'll drop . . .*

I didn't say any of that to Mam.

'Can we have a dog?'

That's what I said to Mam. It was an unexpected question but, once it had popped into my mind and straight out of my mouth, I knew it was precisely what I wanted. I wasn't sure where the idea had come from – it seemed to have been conjured as suddenly from nowhere as a genie from a lamp. Celyn and I had talked about what fun it would be to own a dog but . . .

'Dog! Dog!' Sioned called excitedly from the top step.

'Oh, for crying out loud!' groaned Mam. 'Now see what you've started.'

Once I'd got the idea of a pet dog into my mind, it wouldn't go away. I nagged Mam about it – almost every day.

'I'm not as green as I'm cabbage looking,' Mam said. 'Dogs are a lot of work. I need a dog to look after about as much as I need a hole in the head. Having you and Sioned in the house creates enough havoc, thank you.'

'I'll take care of it, Mam. It'll be no trouble . . .'

'Then there's the cost of food . . . we're not made of money . . . and dogs need exercise. Who's going to take it for walks . . . not me, I can tell you. I've got a life to lead . . .'

'I'll take it for walks . . . every time, Mam. You wouldn't have to do a thing . . .'

'And they need proper training . . .'

'I'll train it, Mam. I'll get a book and learn all about it. You wouldn't know it was here. It'd be the best-behaved dog in town, in Wales, in Europe, in the world, in the galaxy, in the universe. It'd be the most wonderful dog ever. Go on, Mam. What d'you say?'

But Mam wouldn't answer. I thought that was a good sign. I took that as a plus. Usually, when Mam says 'no' she means 'no'.

'Going on and on won't do any good,' she says. 'It'll just turn me being cross into me being even more cross.'

I nagged Dad too as we licked our ice creams on Sunday afternoons. It was rather mean of me because I knew Dad felt guilty – about not living with us any more – about all the stuff that had happened. I didn't let feeling mean stop me, though. I was determined.

'Please, Dad! If you tell Mam it's a good idea . . . well . . . she might agree.'

'I don't think your mother's going to take any notice of me, Hedd. I think those days are over . . .'

'Mmmm . . .'

My dad had changed. There was no getting away from it – he was definitely different. I'd still get vivid flashbacks of the terrible power he used to hold over us. Lightning pictures of his past behaviour:

ZAP   POW   BANG

would still haunt me. Those awful images, those murderous grenade-burst, shell-blitz, bomb-blasts of action:

ZAP   POW   BANG

would still sometimes explode across my dreams. Then my dreams would spin way out of control and change into nightmares.

You don't forget, do you? That stuff stays with you. I suppose . . . probably . . . it'll never completely go away. But I'd learnt to toss my head, lift my chin, move forward rather than dwell on all that distress. I wasn't about to let that . . . mess . . . that rubbish time distract me from my latest quest.

'Mmmm . . . but, Dad . . . what about for my birthday? You could . . . not tell exactly . . . you could . . . suggest . . . to Mam that I should have a dog for my birthday, couldn't you? If I was really good and deserved it, I mean . . .'

Sioned nagged too – when she remembered – if she saw a dog in the street or on a TV programme. Sioned was only copying me. She wasn't head over heels in love with the idea of having a dog as I was. A real dog . . . it's almost the same as a special friend, isn't it? Dogs are more fond and faithful than other pets, aren't they? Take cats, for example. Cats are quite stuck up and independent and don't care about you. Mam had tried to persuade me I'd be happy with a cat.

'Cats aren't so much trouble as dogs,' Mam claimed.

I wasn't at all interested in a cat. Dogs are lively and intelligent and . . . fun. Dogs aren't as gormless as gerbils, for example. Mam had already attempted to palm me off with a gerbil.

'Gerbils are nocturnal,' I explained to Mam patiently. 'So they're really, really boring all day long. We've got some at school and they're useless. Gerbils are an excuse for a pet. Gerbils are so-o not as good as a dog. There's no comparison!'

Mam was a trier – I'll give her that. She tried to entice me with the notion of a budgie, a tortoise, a rabbit, a guinea pig, a goldfish – as if – and even a stick insect. She was on a loser with all of them. I was passionate about a dog. Sioned would've happily had any of those pets. Sioned would've probably have been content with some toy animal she could lug around with her – especially if it was fluffy, particularly if it was pink. But I'd really got my teeth into the idea of having a pet dog and I wasn't about to let it go. Mam said I was like a dog myself . . . a dog with a bone. Dad said I reminded him of Mam – the way I went on. Neither of them said it angrily. They sounded more . . . resigned. So that gave me hope. I took that as a plus. I kept up the pressure.

I nagged right through September as the last local agricultural shows took place and the autumn term began. It was exciting to start at the comp and go on the bus with all the other boys. It was a laugh on the bus – but I didn't let any of that divert me from my campaign. I nagged as the final tourists – the old and crumbly ones – left the beaches and Mam continued to make plans for her new life without Dad. I nagged as October arrived and the first chills set in. I nagged Mam. I nagged Dad . . . whenever I could get a word in between him telling me how he was putting mouse guards on the hives and how he was feeding the bees with sugar to keep them going over the winter.

'What sort of dog would you chose?' asked Celyn. 'If you could chose any dog you wanted, what would it be?'

'A labrador,' I'd said at once.

I'd fantasized about dogs for so long that I knew the answer immediately. 'A golden or a black one would be fine. A golden or a black one would be more than OK, of course . . . but . . . but the cherry on the cake would be chocolate. A chocolate coloured labrador.'

Chapter 9

My birthday's at the end of October. Mistletoe made me a special cake and we had strawberry jelly to keep Sioned happy – although, when you've just turned twelve, jelly's not such a thrill. Dad came and joined us for tea and then Mam, Dad and me went to the cinema. We took Aled and Celyn with us. Mistletoe stayed at home to look after Sioned. She's a hopeless fidget in films – even ones that are supposed to be suitable for her. Dad says Sioned's 'got ants in her pants' when she won't sit still. Mistletoe had Steffan as well – to give Aled's mam a break – and so Sioned didn't feel left out. I had birthday presents too, of course . . . and they were suitable and thoughtful and everyone was more than kind to me . . . but I didn't get a dog. I gave up. I stopped nagging about it. I knew that I should be grateful for everything I did have. Life had been worse, after all, much worse – and at least nobody had bought me a gerbil.

The evenings were drawing in. Dark fell swiftly and Celyn and I couldn't skateboard after school as we used to. We were still putting in some practice though. If the weather was OK on Saturday afternoons, we'd often join in with Aled, Owain and Josh down on the square. They'd throw down their sharpest moves – then we'd throw down ours. They let us use their ramp. First we dropped in frontside. As we went down the incline, we'd bend at our hips and knees and compress the board for speed. As we came up the transition, we'd extend our knees and keep our arms out for balance. We got the hang of it. We progressed from fakies and flips to some aerial stunts. We'd lean down and grab at the boards to give us more control. We'd all try out each other's new moves. We were all getting there . . . but . . . have you any idea who was the best of us, any clue as to who outshone the rest of us? You've got it! Celyn was a whirlygig. Celyn was greased lightning. Celyn was the star.

The short November and December days sped by. On Bonfire Night, the town always has a carnival parade that ends with fireworks and a huge beacon-blaze of a bonfire on the beach. Mistletoe and Mam dressed in their posh summer-show hats and pretended they were puppeteers working Sioned and Steffan as puppets. Sioned was dressed as a pink fairy – so she was over the moon and extra-pink with pleasure – and Steffan was Merlin – or a sort of tiny, tumbling Son of Merlin.

'Whizz, whizz, wizard!' Steffan shouted, all the way down the hill to the beach. He brandished his wand dangerously.

Sioned had our battered, sparkling star attached with sticky tape to her fairy wand.

'Twinkle, twinkle!' she sang all through the town. She poked and prodded people with her wand if they got in her way.

Their over-the-top excitement made everyone laugh and they won the Fancy Dress Group Prize. Mistletoe and Mam kept control by attaching the two of them to their own hands by cords which looked just like puppet strings. Reins would have been more like it, if you ask me.

Celyn led the parade with a joggling display – running and juggling at the same time.

Aled, Josh, Owain and I had made a huge guy together. We wheeled it down to the beach in Sioned's pushchair. The guy slumped untidily in his seat. He was ragged and patched and wore one of Dad's old hats. Mistletoe had given us a grotesque mask for him – red-cheeked, hook-nosed with bulging eyes. We'd all thought it was a hoot but, when we got him on the sands, I took a good look at him in the flickering firelight. He suddenly seemed to . . . shift . . . come to life. One arm fell loose from the push-chair and swung to and fro. All at once, he reminded me of . . . Mr Punch on the night I first saw him and of . . . my nightmare dad. I was almost sure he winked at me. I shook my head to destroy the image. I wasn't going back there.

'One, two, three . . .'

Aled and I took hold of the arms, Owain and Josh had hold of the legs and we swung him high, launched him into the flames. Everyone whooped. The guy had been stuffed with old newspaper and flared in seconds, was gone in minutes. Over, finished, done with – dust and ashes.

Then the Catherine wheels out-spun Sioned's star and the rockets whooshed up – bursting into flowery showers of red and gold, silver and green. They

114

illuminated the whole town, flared across the bay. You could probably have seen them from as far away as Enlli.

'Whizz twinkle, twinkle whizz!' shouted Sioned and Steffan as they charged round in circles, stirring the night sky with their wands. 'Abracadabra, abracadabra!'

Everyone was as giggly and giddy and glowing as a merry-go-round. Celyn and I joined hands and turned, faster and faster, like a couple in the centre of a twmpath. When I finally stood still again, the harbour rocked like a cradle under a canopy of light and even the moon seemed to croon softly to me – a lullaby of happiness.

'Never mind . . . Christmas is coming,' mothers consoled their tired-out children when the fire had finally died down and the last sparkler had sparked. We all trudged back up to the town. 'Only forty-nine shopping days to go!'

At school, they wanted Year 7 volunteers to sign up to perform at the Christmas concert. You had to do a turn – either alone or with friends. They kept announcing it in assembly – trying to drum up support. Some of the girls were keen and put their names down immediately. Gwenllian, Nia, Catrin and Kelly were rehearsing their folk dancing number every break time from about November 5th onwards. Ffion was eager to play the piano because she was already doing Grade 6 and had cups in a cabinet at home. Rhian was going to treat us to a poetry reading of her own work. Sian and Roxanne wanted to sing a duet. Sian wanted to do 'Myfanwy' because it was her mam's favourite. Roxanne said that 'Myfanwy' was dreary as dishwater and about as stylish as a tea-cosy. She was holding out for something in the charts. Roxanne told Sian that, if they sang something trendy, they'd have to be allowed to paint their nails and put highlights in their hair and dress like proper pop-princesses. Sian insisted on sounding out Ms Probert. Why do girls do that? Go buttering up teachers, making a great to-do? Do they live on this planet? Anyone could have told them Ms P. would think Sian Goody-Two-Shoes Morris had the right idea and that Roxanne Davies was a potential bad influence and that they probably shouldn't be allowed to sit together after all.

Sure enough, Ms P. sucked her cheeks in.

'Popular is acceptable,' said Ms P., 'but . . .' and at this point she directed the most withering glare I've ever seen towards Roxanne, 'the lyrics obviously must be suitable and costumes obviously must be . . . likewise.'

Adults and their looks, eh? You have to be more direct with someone like Roxanne. You have to be specific . . . tell it like it is. Roxanne's the type of girl who can easily interpret a glare as the go-ahead – especially if it suits her. I got the message loud and clear . . . but I was pretty certain it went sailing right over Roxanne's head. Anyway, Ms P. should have guessed that her notion of suitable and Roxanne's were – obviously – going to be adrift.

At least a show-down between Roxanne and Ms P. will make the concert more interesting, I thought.

116

Not many boys were coming forward to volunteer. Gareth was going to give us another taste of the recitation he'd done for the school eisteddfod and . . . that was about it.

'Come along, boys,' Ms Probert chivied us one morning at registration. 'You're letting the side down.'

We gazed at her. No one put a hand up.

'Right. I'm making a note of the six boys who are in the choir. You can get together and rustle up a musical interlude for us.'

'Aw . . . Miss!'

'No arguments . . . now . . . who else have we got? There must be some hidden talents surely? A light lurking under a bushel . . .'

'Rhodri can tell jokes, Miss.'

'But they're rude, Miss.'

The two boys either side of Rhodri nudged him and Rhodri smirked.

'Yes, Miss, there's the one about ...'

'Thank you, Rhodri. I don't think jokes are quite what we're after. Let's see . . . Hedd, what about you?'

'He's been learning to juggle, Miss, and he dresses up like a clown.'

Oh, thanks a bunch, Rhodri, I thought.

He'd obviously been miffed at being passed over as a comedian – but why had he landed me in it instead?

'I can't really juggle at all, Ms Probert. I'm useless . . . truly I am.'

I tried to nip the suggestion in the bud.

'Now, now. I'm sure you're simply being modest.

A juggling clown . . . that'll be excellent and so . . . different. I've put your name on my list, so there's no backing out of it.'

'Oh Miss! It's supposed to be voluntary. That's so unfair!'

But it was too late. She was off through the door of the classroom in two shakes of a lamb's tail, with her rotten list clutched firmly in her hand . . . and with my name on it.

'I'll help you,' said Celyn when I told her the bad news. 'I'll go over all the moves with you.'

'But you've tried to teach me before and I'm hopeless. A baboon with his arms tied behind his back would give a more competent juggling display than I ever could.'

'Faint heart never won fair lady,' murmured Mam, as she wandered by distractedly with a sewing basket. My mam seemed preoccupied at that time . . . head in the clouds, walking on air . . . anyhow, not quite with us. I stared after her retreating back. Parents, I ask you! If it's not one thing, it's another . . .

'I don't want to win a fair lady,' I muttered. 'I want to be let off the hook. I want a reprieve.'

From then on, every night after school, I went over to Celyn's house and we practised imitating the moves of juggling sequences. At least it was too dark for skateboarding – otherwise I'd have been even more indignant about Ms P. organizing my life for me. Teachers! Where are they coming from? One minute they're telling you to listen precisely to what they're saying – the next they're saying 'voluntary' but meaning 'compulsory'.

Dad often walked me across to the Midwinters' and collected me later. He was spending quite a few evenings at our house around then – helping Mam redecorate the front room. That was something. It was more peaceful at Celyn's than at home – what with the sawing and hammering and so on. Our house was a hive of activity and Mam was smiling smiles as wide and open as the bay, laughing aloud, the soft hum of a song always on her lips. Even Sioned's determination to get involved didn't appear to dampen Mam's spirits.

'I've a project in mind,' Mam said mysteriously if I questioned her. 'I'm taking control of my life. It'll soon be Christmas and then New Year . . . a new year, a new start.'

'December's wrap-up time for the bees,' Dad had told her. 'I've insulated the hives with sawdust against the cold and there's nothing much else needed until March. That means I've got more time to spare. So . . . so I'll be happy to lend a hand, Marian. If you want me to, that is . . . It's the least I can do.'

So there they were – working away side by side and making more noise than a herd of clog-dancing elephants. I left them to it.

Celyn was true to her word and she trained me hard. Every evening, I stood behind her and mirrored the movements of her hands in order to learn the juggling routines. She added plenty of other movements too – leaps and turns, stretches and ducks

119

– sometimes it felt as if I was learning a dance. There were also facial expressions and extravagant bows that she wanted me to copy.

'You're going to be dressed as a clown,' she reminded me. 'Parts of the act have got to appear funny and full of . . . razzle-dazzle.'

'It's all very well learning this stuff,' I grumbled. 'I've not so much as tossed a single ball yet. You wait until we start on the real juggling. It'll be chaos, carnage.'

I stood slightly forward on my toes, knees bent, palms up, wrists loose. My hands and forearms described inward and outward circles in the air. I focused my eyes at the correct point – the top of where a ball's arc would be, if I ever got as far as throwing anything, that is. Prompted by Celyn, I made the calls – first for a simple two-ball, right-hand exchange. I fitted my actions to suit:

Left hand	–	'Throw!'
Right hand	–	'Throw!'
Right hand	–	'Catch!'
Left hand	–	'Catch!'

I called more elaborate patterns. I called out the numbers of balls – imagined them flying through the air before me: 'One! Two! Three! Four! Five! Six! Seven! Eight! Nine!'

She's completely lost the plot here, I thought.

'Celyn,' I protested. 'There's absolutely no way I'll manage nine genuine balls in the air at the same time!'

'Trust me,' she said.

So I did. I pretended to juggle with my eyes closed. I tried to show I was juggling with one hand. I imitated all the throws and sequences Celyn had done on the beach. I acted vamping balls from one hand to another and clawing them from the air. Then we added more complex body throws, drop-bounces and force-bounces.

'Er . . . Celyn . . . I don't want to be a complete wimp but . . . are you intending to make me try to juggle with balls that . . . that . . . bounce? ! ? ! ?'

I was appalled. I was getting the hang of the actions – but what good was that going to do me?

'Oh yes,' said Celyn, 'balls are certainly going to be involved. In fact, Mistletoe is going to let you use our very best, state of the art, silicon rubber, stage balls. They're precision-made to feel and look wonderful. They'll bounce amazingly high!'

'Oh, terrific! Thanks so much for that! You've boosted my confidence no end . . . When do we begin rehearsing with them? The concert's next week and I'm sure I'll never manage to get it all together in time.'

'Patience,' said Celyn. 'Trust me.'

So I did. What alternative had I got?

Celyn told me to bring Aled along and she taught us some moves for duo juggling: sharing the balls side by side, stealing a pattern from your partner from beside them, stealing a pattern from your partner on the runaround. Celyn made us mime it all – pull faces, pretend to trip each other up. We appeared to toss balls at lightning speed, fast as a thunder shower. We were performing like a couple of ace jugglers. We were performing like a couple of clowns – and it was slick and it was hilarious.

Aled was far from delighted to find himself roped in – and even less so when he saw the circus costume Mistletoe planned to lend him. It involved a seriously ruffled shirt and yellow sateen trousers. But he hung in there, stuck with me like a true friend.

'In for a penny, in for a pound,' he sighed, tightening his lilac cummerbund.

'We'll never be able to do this prancing about and grimacing like gargoyles and wearing of . . . of panto disguises . . . and yet still manage to throw and catch balls at the same time!' both of us wailed at Celyn when she allowed us a rare break. 'And we've hardly any time left. When are we going to learn how to really juggle?'

'Trust me,' said Celyn.

So we did. One evening, she asked us to bring Owain and Josh along too. They watched our show and roared with laughter and whistled and stamped their feet.

'But . . . but where are the juggling balls?' they asked at the end. 'Haven't you got around to including any balls yet?'

Celyn took them over to the corner of the room to show them the extra-special juggling balls, the dreaded juggling balls, the juggling balls Aled and I knew we'd never cope with. Celyn whispered to Owain and Josh and gave them the balls to take care of. There were boxes of them – boxes and boxes.

'Wait a minute!' I protested. 'How can we be

expected to juggle if Owain and Josh have taken away the equipment we need? And ...'

My mouth went dry as I took in the stacks of boxes in the boys' arms.

'And how many balls . . . precisely . . . are you expecting us to use at once?'

Then Celyn explained. And we were glad we'd trusted her. The concert was going to be a breeze.

On the big night, the school hall was packed – a sell out.

'All credit to your organizational skills, Ms Probert.'

'Thank you, Headmaster,' simpered Ms P.

'All credit to being a bossy-boots and a battleaxe, Ms Pain-in-the-bum,' muttered Roxanne. Ms P. had re-written the words to the song she and Sian had chosen and insisted their dance routine was 'closer to gymnastics' and therefore had to be done in regulation tracksuits. Roxanne had said it cramped their style.

Ms P. had said: 'Like it or lump it, take it or leave it, girls.'

Sian and Roxanne were taking it.

The audience clapped Gareth's recitation politely and managed not to fall asleep during Rhian's very long and very incomprehensible poem – which didn't sound like a poem at all to me, I must say. There should be something in the sound of a poem that tells you it's a poem – something . . . musical . . . if you get my drift. Rhian's poem had no rhythm, didn't sing in my ears, and that really depressed me. I sat in the wings with my head in my hands. Rhian's the sort of poet who gives poetry a bad name, if you want my opinion. Her mam, her dad and her mam-gu stood up at the end, clapping fit to burst a blood vessel and shouting: 'Encore! Encore!'

Thankfully the rest of the audience managed to stare them down and Ms P. – credit where credit's due – scurried quickly across the stage to elbow Rhian off and announce the final act. The moment of truth . . . or, as Ms P. put it: 'The moment you've all been waiting for . . .'

Aled and I were on.

We went down a storm. I suppose anything must have come as a relief after Rhian, but the audience loved us. They were with us right from the start in imagining we were juggling so fast and so high that the balls were invisible. They participated in the effect by cheering and gasping and oh-ing and ah-ing at suitable points. But the real show-stopper came – appropriately – right at the end. As Aled and I took our final bows – Josh and Owain released nets above the stage and balls rained down around us. The audience roared. All the balls they'd had to imagine during our act were suddenly there in front of them – as if we'd truly been juggling after all. Josh and Owain bowled in more balls from the wings and Aled and I made things funnier by zooming to all corners of the stage trying to capture them. Balls bounded and bounced everywhere. The whole audience was on its feet – jumping in the aisles, clapping and catching. We brought the house down.

So – what more can I tell you?

We all had Christmas Day together. Dad came down from the caravan and Mistletoe and Celyn came from across the harbour – even Aled and Steffan wandered over for part of the afternoon. Everyone was squashed like sardines into our back dining room – but no one got stressed, no one became angry. It was a great Christmas – way, way-out-of-sight better than last year.

Mam has taken over the front room for her millinery business. There are now shelves all around the walls displaying the most incredible hats imaginable. In the bay window, there's a tall wire triangle of shelving bedecked with an arrangement of green hats. They're ornamented with miniature baubles of cranberry-glass and opal beads. With their beading, feathers, frills and flounces – they look like the best Christmas tree ever. Mam says she's already planning her next window display – so we'll have wonderful decorations to enjoy all through the year. Outside there's a sign Mistletoe painted for Mam. Bright red letters edged with gold on a deep, deep green board. The script carves into twirls and curlicues to spell:

Marionette's

That's what Mam's calling her new business – partly, she says, because there's an echo of her name in the word and partly because it holds a reminder of Mistletoe and her puppets and the difference she made. Words . . . names . . . they're fascinating, aren't they?

Dad says the building at the Honey Farm was once a chapel called Bethlehem. Bethlehem's a good word too. It's got a soft sound – three peaceful syllables on your tongue. Dad's planted a holly tree in our back garden for us. It's shaped like a giant witch's hat, or a wizard's, and festooned in berries. We draped it with fairy lights for Christmas and put Sioned's star on top. Even when the decorations are taken down, the holly tree will be with us forever – to remind us of Celyn.

Now all the glitz and celebrations are over, the Midwinters say it's time for them to move on. Celyn tells me they've never-ever stayed in one place – from midwinter to midwinter – for so long. We've been lucky to have them. I've been fortunate to know them. Once, I would have panicked at their leaving. Once, scary thoughts, memories of dark times, all my uncertainties – those old black crows – would have flown back to surround me. Now? I'll miss them . . . but we won't lose them, we'll always be in touch. I'm sure Celyn and Mistletoe will keep their promises and be constantly writing us letters and notes and postcards . . . and so on. I'm going to keep a diary all next year – from midwinter to midwinter – so I can remember everything that happens and tell Celyn when I write back.

Next year Josh and Owain, Aled and I plan to start a campaign for a proper skateboard park in the town. About time too, I think. Some girls from school – Nia and Gwenllian, Catrin and Kelly – are going to make posters for us. Celyn will want to know how we get on.

Sioned's grown up a lot – and she's certainly not so clingy and definitely not such a tap. She's allowed to start school next year. Sioned and Steffan, those two little kids, can you believe it? They're both horribly excited already and talk of nothing else. Mam shakes her head.

'Those teachers don't know what they've got coming, poor dabs!' she says. Then she grins to herself.

Who knows if we'll all live happily ever after? Life's not a fairy tale, is it? When you're my age, you know things are harder, more complex, than that. Things that happen stay with you, things that happen affect you forever . . . shape who you are. At least those other midwinters – those dark and desperate sadnesses – seem to have left me at last. The crows continue to flutter and flap about our chimney pots, caw in the trees next door. But now . . . now I'm just as likely to hear the seabirds calling and notice the glint of light on their wings as they soar and swoop over the town. Occasionally, when the evening sun streams across our bay like honey, gilding Enlli and Snowdonia and the harbour, sometimes then even the grotty crows' nests glimmer. They sway, juggled by sea breeze, special and mysterious as great bunches, magical balls, of mistletoe. Things change, don't they? You can view things in so many different ways. I suppose . . . I suppose I'm moving on too.

Tomorrow, we're all going to wave Mistletoe and Celyn off in the removal van they've hired. It's loaded up and ready outside their house. I can see Mistletoe from my window – standing for one last time on the harbour wall – just where the 'pepper pot' used to be. She's standing there straight and sturdy yet slim and subtle as a wand. She's gazing towards Enlli. The sea is midwinter: grey, bone-white but sparkling, sparking.

I'm sitting in my bedroom, cwtshed high in the roof of our house. It remains one of my favourite places to be – and it's even better at this moment. At my feet is a dog basket, lined with a red cushion that's patterned with holly leaves – to remind me of Celyn – and sprigs of mistletoe – to remind me of her mother. Curled up in the basket is a puppy, a chocolate labrador puppy called Ivy. She was the Midwinters' farewell and Christmas present to me. I've promised to train her and walk her and Mrs Price-Owen has said I can start a paper round – so that'll help pay to feed her. Dad braved the newsagents and asked her for me. Dad – my hero! He took Mrs Price-Owen some honey as a peace offering.

So that'll be me next year . . . skateboarding and school, paper round and diary writing, keeping in touch with Celyn, putting the world to rights with my friends, enjoying my very own pet dog . . . it's good to have things to look forward to, isn't it? I wonder what adventures the future holds? I feel I'm balancing here on the year's rim – knees and hips bent, feet shoulder width apart, arms outstretched, leaning forward – about to drop in on its turning.